The Way We Wind

Halli Starling

Halli Starling Books

Contents

Dedication

Thanks to my early readers: Cayla, Anna, Clanky, Katie Gray, and Jeannie Marschall.

The incredible character art of Bren & Elodie, and Clark & Jasper, was done by Cayla (@veranox on Twitter). Cayla's been a friend for some years now, and she makes incredible art pieces that capture the feel of a moment and the embodiment of characters, as if she ripped them from my mind and breathed life into them via her pen.

Author's Note

Readers sometimes ask if certain things in my books are real – like the tabletop game "Dungeon Delve" in my novella *When He Beckons*. (Sadly, it is not real, as much as I would like it to be.)

In this novella, "ghost trails" are an amalgamation of stories about spectral hauntings and ley lines brimming with power. I am not a believer in the paranormal or supernatural, but I can absolutely see and understand where the fascination comes from. Believing that our loved ones linger near us after their deaths is a powerful, often comforting, image.

While "ghost trails" are a figment of my authorial imagination, as is the town of Haven, Michigan, the abandoned copper mining towns in the Upper Peninsula of the state are not. When an 1841 geologist's report described the massive copper deposits under the ground on which the Chippewa tribe lived, spectators rushed to the area. You can imagine what happened to the native peoples of that place, and many other places in what is now known as Keweenaw County. Dozens of copper mines were quickly slapped together, and around the mines shanty towns practically erupted from the ground. When the copper veins dried up, the towns had no other business to support those living there, and the towns were soon abandoned. Some of those towns still stand today, while others have been ground down to rubble of a handful of buildings, or even only a few graves.

So while this area – and its history – are real, the story Clark tells Jasper is also a figment of my imagination. I blame too many history books and podcasts, as I don't feel the tragic story seems too far-fetched. If you're curious about the ghost towns of Michigan's Upper Peninsula, I did an episode of The Human Exception Podcast on this very topic (episode 72).

I want to also note Bren's difficulties with her anxiety and depression, as their impact may be outsized compared to their triggers, namely the viral video which causes her to spiral. Anxiety and depression look and feel different on different people. For instance, the mere thought I might be late to an appointment makes my heart race and my hands clammy. For others, public speaking may cause a similar, or more intense reaction. There are many, many reasons why someone suffers from these conditions, and Bren's story is her own. Her struggles may not look like yours, but they are still important to talk about, and no one's mental health struggles should feel as though they're "not enough" of an excuse or justification.

Character Art

Elodie & Bren

Jasper & Clark

Art by Cayla (@veranox on Twitter)

Chapter One

Bren looked up from her phone with a frown. "Ugh."

"Ugh, what?"

She cleared her throat, then affected a slightly higher pitch before reading the opening line of the message she'd just received. "You know, your name in Gaelic means *raven*."

There was a bark of laughter from the kitchen before Clark appeared around the open doorway, two steaming mugs in hand. "Did they ask if your hair is really that dark?" her brother asked as Brenna stifled a snort, which turned into a cough. "Real smooth, Bren."

"Just get over here," she said between coughs, swinging her legs off the couch so Clark had a place to sit. She scrolled through the ridiculously long message on her dating app. "No mention of my *black as night* hair, or whatever the last girl's line was." Bren tossed the phone beside her, secretly hoping it would get lost between the gray cushions and pinstriped yellow and orange pillows Clark had made a few years back. "I'm about to shut down my account. It's worthless."

Clark took a sip of his tea, winced, and sat the mug down before leaning back. Bren immediately handed him a pillow, which he held against his stomach as he stared off in thought. "You could always try that speed dating thing again down at Flannery's."

"I could. But if you recall, it didn't go well last time." Or the time before that, or the first time. It wasn't like Jackson Park wasn't open about its queerness - every year the city held a massive Pride parade, and it was always on those travel blog lists of "Best LGBTQ towns in the US". In a city this size, you could easily move around like all the other nameless citizens and never once worry about bumping into someone you knew. At least, that was the case for most people. You could congregate at the gay bars, go to Pride, go dancing, and all the while meet new people. Maybe take one home.

But Bren was a little stuck for "local" options, all because of that damn commercial.

Clark's voice broke into her thoughts. "If you're blaming everything on the commercial..."

Bren scoffed. "If? Oh sure, made the greenhouse thrive but it really put a damper on my dating life." Her put-on sarcasm made Clark splutter a laugh in his tea. "You are really mean, brother."

"I'm not mean." He paused to push up his glasses. "I'm realistic. And besides, we both know you could barely leave the house after all that. It feels like it's just now going back to normal. But Flannery's attracts a big crowd from the hotels and conference center. You never know. Not everyone has seen the video. It could be a good night for you."

How could she not smile at that? Clark's ever-hopeful sense of optimism, even if couched behind a self-labeled "realist", was one of the big ways they were different. It was always a nice reminder that even though they were twins, they were still their own people. "You know what? You're right. I should try again."

Clark didn't look surprised at all. "Good! You are gonna have better luck this time, I just know it."

She grinned at him as he pushed up his glasses again. "Your intuition tell you that?"

"It's the spirits," he replied back instantly with a wiggle of his fingers. "They send me messagessssss!"

Now she was laughing, more at the wide-eyed look on his face than his goofy "spooky" voice. "Do that for the kids at the library Halloween party and they'll love it."

"I'm planning on it, even if it's a long way off. No scares for the toddler storytime, but we always get a bunch of families coming in for the party later in the day. Gotta spook it up a bit for the older kids." Clark gulped down the rest of his tea and glanced at her mug. "More?"

"Nah. I'm gonna head to bed."

"I'll clean up, don't worry."

Bren stood, stretched, then reached down to ruffle her brother's shaggy black hair. "I never do."

He huffed and scraped his hair back into place. "That is the biggest lie..."

Bren grinned, waved, and headed down the hallway for her boots and coat. The little mud room off the kitchen wasn't more than a narrow passageway that led to the covered patio, but it was one of her favorite spots in the house. Clark had way too many coats and jackets and shoes, but at least he could keep them somewhat organized here. It was homey and cluttered and smelled like leather from the dress shoes Clark wore to work.

She plucked her jacket off a hook and shoved her feet into her rain boots. "Night, you two," she said softly as she ran her fingers over the picture to the left of the door. The couple in the photo were leaning against a pier railing, the man's temple pressed into the woman's as they smiled wide and bright. Behind them, the ocean was as smooth as glass, reflecting the majestic pinks and purples of oncoming twilight.

Bren always thought she and Clark looked like the perfect amalgamation of their parents' features, especially in this photo. Their dad's black hair, their mom's slightly upturned nose; but the differences were there, too. Clark got Dad's dimples and she had Mom's thick eyebrows.

Bren stared at the photo a moment longer than normal, her gaze lingering on its yellowed edges. They really needed to buckle down and get all the family photos properly archived. Age seemed to be catching up with all of their family's memories. Stairs creaked that didn't used to, some of the wallpaper in the den was finally peeling away from the wall. Clark was getting gray hair almost in the same spot she had discovered her first few silver strands.

All of it was fading slowly, growing distant as the tide of time threatened to wash the more vibrant details away.

"Thought you were going to bed."

Bren ran her finger over the photo once more. "Got stuck, I guess."

"Yeah." Clark came to stand beside her. "I do that sometimes, too."

She rubbed the heel of her palm into her forehead before finally saying, "Okay, now I'm going to bed." Bren squeezed her brother's arm, waved when he said goodnight once more, then headed out to the barn.

Converted years ago by her parents, the "barn" had once been an actual working barn on their family farm. But when her parents had bought the farm back from distant relatives when she and Clark were only toddlers, they'd set about fixing up everything. It had taken years; the sounds of sawing and hammering, the scent of paint on the air had all seemed persistent. But her mother's pet project had been the barn, even as old and decayed as it was. Their mother had turned it into a plant nursery, with a living space above originally meant for out-of-town guests if the main house ran out of room.

With spring approaching, the nursery was laden with tiny green sprigs of herbs and a few runs of ferns. Bags of soil, trowels, gloves, buckets, and more littered the space on the ground floor. But her space above was its own little world and Bren kept it as uncluttered as possible.

Living above the nursery had been Bren's idea, one she never regretted even when memories of their mother pushed their way to the forefront. She'd needed separation from the main house. Sometimes being surrounded by their parents' things *ached*. But her brother? Clark was the nester, the young "old" man shuffling around in slippers and a housecoat, a mug of tea always in hand. The house's chipped wood tables and faded paint, rambling, overflowing bookshelves, and frayed rugs all worked for him. The house was the biggest reminder of their parents, and it helped Clark to keep them close. Over the years they'd fixed broken shelves and replaced old appliances, but the house was very much the same as when their parents had first renovated it.

Being twins didn't mean their minds worked the same way, and her grieving process was a trickle of sand compared to her brother's.

Once upstairs, Bren flicked on the light over the sink and poured herself a glass of wine. It was going to be one of those nights, she could tell; the kind where her mind kept sleep at bay with a firm hand. Maybe Clark was right. Maybe it was time to get back out there, try dating again. Surely eighteen months was enough time, especially given the short attention span of the Internet, for everyone to forget about the "hero plant lady", right?

Common sense, and the speed at which information moved nowadays, had to mean no one remembered that commercial. There was no way. Bren *knew* things had largely returned to normal because her days had the proper ebb and flow to them, now that they were no longer interrupted by random customers asking for pictures with her to post on their social feeds.

She'd been an accidental blip on the radar. Everything was *fine*. But she didn't feel fine. The meds helped some; the talk therapy more. Anxiety had been a silent, ever-watchful presence in Bren's life since far before their father's death when they'd been kids. *It just happened sometimes*, Bren remembered her pediatrician telling her parents. *Some kids are wired for it, others aren't.*

And even today, Bren found that incredibly unfair.

It was only once the wine was set on her bedside table and she was propped up against a few pillows, book in hand, did Bren stop to think about deleting the dating app from her phone. It was bad enough being a demisexual woman on an app where a single photo seemed to invite the weirdest creeps possible, but this had been the last app she'd swore she'd try.

Staring at the little icon on the screen and its message alert notification made her throat close up. But even then, it was so tempting to check the three new messages.

Maybe one of them would be from someone interesting, who wasn't pervy or weird; someone who didn't know who she was but liked the picture of her with the ferns in the greenhouse.

Don't. Don't do it. You know what Clark would say.

Just delete it. Go back to Flannery's, let Nica tease you as she pours you a beer, meet some new people. Be brave. Stop thinking that everything will fall apart or end badly.

Bren deleted the app with a satisfying *click*, drank the last of the wine, and read until midnight before falling into a dreamless sleep.

Chapter Two

The older man's chatter rolled over Clark, letting him keep his focus on the computer screen while also keeping an eyeline on the woman roaming the stacks. The customer in front of him was a regular, and he often nattered on about this or that thing happening in his neighborhood. It didn't really take any effort on Clark's end to pause or hum as politely as possible.

But the woman in the stacks was suspected of stealing from the library and Clark had to admit to some curiosity about the book currently in her hands. It was a large natural sciences guide, and well....if she found room in her gray pants for it, he'd be tempted to let her walk away with it. To the winner go the spoils and all that.

"Anyways, I told Felicity that she should bring the grandkids over for lunch on Sunday but she's afraid it will rain. Do you think it will rain?"

"Hmm, it is that time of year. Unpredictable." Clark navigated to one last search page, hoping to find the obscure title the man had asked about. Another quick glance to the stacks told him....yep, she was definitely trying to fit that book down her pants.

"Would you excuse me for just a second?" Clark asked the older patron, not waiting for the man to nod and keep rambling. He quickly walked over to the copier where his colleague May was talking with someone from IT, a younger woman named Natasha. "Hate to interrupt," he said before jerking a thumb back to the woman in the stacks. "Could you see to her, May? Mr. Graves is bending my ear and I..."

May rubbed her hands together. "Say no more! Which camera is better, three or four?"

"Probably four, but maybe Natasha can assist if the woman puts up a fuss."

"Oh, she will." May looked delighted. "I've been waiting to bust her since last week and I nearly caught her trying to walk out with one of our acrylic pamphlet holders. Who steals that kind of thing?"

Natasha snickered while Clark shook his head and said, "Well, you know the drill. Discreet, please."

"Done and done." May gave him a thumb's up and then strode off. "No police needed, I swear."

May's last statement had proven false, unfortunately.

They wound up needing the police once the woman refused to leave, but that was only after she pulled out a handful of miniature candy bars and threw them at May, hitting his colleague in the eye. And *that* was after May asked for the book back and the woman called her a whore and said the Devil would get her.

Clark's afternoon became a blur of incident reports, phone calls, and several witness statements. The entire thing left him drained at the end of the day, worn down to practically slumping through his front door two hours later than normal. But the scent of rosemary and paprika hit his nose, pulling him to the kitchen.

Clark found a plate left on "warm" in the oven. Bren had already made dinner and left him some.

She did this on occasion, never with any pattern or rhythm. Bren either wanted company or she didn't, but she liked cooking and knowing that her brother ate enough throughout the day. Her silent caretaking never failed to warm his heart.

It'll keep for a few more minutes, he thought as he shuffled through the back hallway to his bedroom. When Mom had passed and they'd settled out of the estate, Clark hadn't felt right taking the master bedroom. That was a little *too* close to sleeping with ghosts, even if all that lingered of their parents had been the house and memories bursting with love. Besides, the guest bedroom at the back of the house had always been his favorite, with its eastern facing windows and sage green curtains. Turning the master bedroom into a sitting room had worked out well, and now it was where he and Bren liked to have game nights with friends or where Bren hosted the greenhouse book club.

Having dinner waiting for him made things feel a little bit better, so Clark found himself smiling as he pulled out fresh pajama pants and an old sweatshirt and turned the shower on full blast. The cranky old water heater banged to life but hot water in this house was a waiting game, so Clark took out his phone and scrolled mindlessly through an article on new thriller books.

DING

The only alert he kept turned on for his phone was for email, so Clark opened the newest message.

Special announcement from the PhantasmaScreams Crew!

Ticket sale alert!

Yes, we have just opened up five more slots on our Philadelphia overnight paranormal tour, but we're so happy to announce that we've got a new SPECIAL tour planned in....

Haven, Michigan!!! OooOOOoooo!

Yes, one of the most haunted places in this lovely northern state is supposedly on the old grounds of a deadly clash between settlers. We'll be camping among some haunted woods!

GET YOUR TICKETS NOW!

Clark didn't hesitate for a second, even as steam fogged the mirror. Haven was only a few hours to the northeast and PhantasmaScreams, his favorite group of ghost hunters, had yet to come to Michigan. He practically ran for his wallet, pulled out his credit card, and purchased his ticket. The ghost hunt was in just over three weeks and while the thought of planning something so late was a little panic-inducing, Clark couldn't get over the fact that he'd get to go at all.

As a knot of excitement bound up in his stomach, he barely noticed the scalding hot shower, his mind far too interested in planning what gear he'd need to take. It was early spring, so the weather would probably be rainy and miserable like all the other days had been. But a few nights spent camping in the chilly air was worth it for the chance to maybe see something out there. His shiver had nothing to do with stepping out into the cool air of the bathroom and everything to do with his intuition screaming at him.

Maybe this time.

Maybe this time you will see something.

It'll be worth it.

"Oh my god, I'm sweating."

Bren fanned Havaa with the board game's instruction sheet. "We can do this. We just need to strategize." She shot the man seated across from her with a pointed look.

"I'm a slutty bisexual, not a board game strategist," Pierre joked before gulping down a mouthful of beer. "Also, we're out of cheese."

"I got it!" Clark shot up from his seat. "I want another slice of that bread before Havaa eats it all."

Havaa stuck out her tongue at him while the others laughed.

A few minutes later, Clark was struggling with the packaging on some gouda. "Scissors," Bren said as she snuck up behind him.

"I'm being reticent."

"I noticed."

Once the cheese was opened, Clark laid it down on the cutting board and began slicing. "I thought you'd be cheesed out after the first spread," he said.

Bren reached out to ruffle his hair, an attempt he managed to dodge. "Impossible. My body is immune to lactose," Bren said while plucking a freshly sliced chunk off the cutting board.

"Lucky you," he groused while Bren plated the cheese. He waited until she was almost done before speaking up. "So hey, I wanted to tell you. I booked another tour and...okay, I know."

To her credit, Bren looked confused. "You know what?"

He shrugged. "That you think my ghost tours are silly."

Bren was silent for a moment before putting the plate down and placing her hands on his shoulders. The look on her face was oddly intense as she asked, "Do you enjoy them?"

Now he was the one confused. "What? Yeah, of course."

"Then that's all that matters." Bren squeezed his shoulders. "When is it?"

"April 5th and 6th."

"That's the weekend of the next Flannery's speed dating thing."

Clark didn't know what to say. He was touched by his sister's words and still a little confused, but now it was because she was smiling like she might actually *enjoy* the speed dating event. "Wouldn't it be funny if we both met someone that weekend?"

Bren let him go and picked up the cheese plate again. "Never say never."

Clark waved a hand in front of her face. "Are you a pod person?"

That got him a sigh and the return of the Bren he knew. "No, I'm just tired of being a fucking bummer all the time."

"A pessimist."

She flipped him off and he laughed. "Fine, a pessimist. I'm trying something new."

Clark took her hand and squeezed it between his own. He'd noticed Bren was gone between eleven and noon every Sunday of late. His chest had burned with pride upon realizing she was going back to therapy. She'd never been anti-therapy for others, but had insisted for years after their parents' deaths that she didn't need it. That she was dealing on her own. And then when she had tried it, Bren had bounced from therapist to therapist, insisting they were just in it for the money. Or angrily huffing about how they wanted to prescribe her even more medications. It had been the one thing his stalwart sister seemed too proud to keep pursuing, and it had almost driven a wedge between them.

He was always the touchy one, so Clark resisted the urge to pull her into a hug and settled for squeezing her hand once more. Bren's lips twitched into a smile and he knew she got the message.

Clark followed her down the hallway and into the room where Pierre and Havaa waited. "Cheese monster slain, I see," Pierre said, grinning. "And while you two were in the kitchen, we figured out the next move."

"Oh, thank fuck," Bren said as she sank into her chair. "Cause it kind of looks like we're..."

"Boned? Yeah, I thought so, too." Havaa pointed to the ocean tiles surrounding the little island they'd spent the last hour carefully cultivating. "If the storm moves in on the next card, there's a thirty-three percent chance of it wiping out the crops. And then another thirty-three percent chance of it causing a landslide. But if we burn our last two luck points-"

Clark hissed. "Dangerous."

Havaa held up a hand. "I know, I know. Totally boned maybe. But just maybe we burn those points, stave off the storm, and survive another round."

Pierre swallowed a bite of cheese before saying, "Brutal but efficient. And when we die, we'll all remember to not listen to Havaa again - ow!" He wiggled another piece of cheese at her. "Pinching is off limits!"

"Not for my cousin, it isn't!"

"Fine, then I declare us to be no longer related."

Clark was too busy laughing at his friends to notice his phone buzzing. The text went unread until the next morning, when Clark woke up with the imprint of his pillow on his cheek and bedhead so bad it made him grimace at his reflection. When he was in the bathroom, his phone buzzed again and, thinking it was Havaa or Pierre, Clark thumbed open the screen.

> **From: May** *Dude did you not c my txt last night? HG was in the library yesterday asking for u!!!! He needs more book recs like the last time.*

Clark groaned. HG, or "Hot Glasses" was a source of some chatter amongst the staff. Clark had met him almost a year ago when he'd been filling in for some of the front desk clerks who were out sick. He'd looked up as someone approached and been confronted by the most beautiful man he'd ever seen in person. Being a professional meant he could keep his cool while the man - tall, honey blonde hair, tattoo of a treble clef on his left index finger, and cheekbones you could cut glass with - filled out an application for a library card.

Clark had stayed totally fine all through the transaction, until the man put out his hand and said, "I'm Jasper."

The voice, all deep and accented with a bit of French, had done something bendy and twisty to Clark's gut, somehow making him think about thick, rich toffee and a cup of good tea all at the same time.

And now, a year and at least fifty book recommendations later, HG - sorry, Jasper - entering the library was an event. And if Jasper didn't ask for or beeline straight to Clark every time, the entire staff would have likely rioted. Clark would have considered joining them.

His stomach doing flip-flops, Clark answered May.

> **From: Clark** *I have that list at my desk. Did you give him something from that?*

From: May *I tried but he said he ALSO had a project he needed assistance with & you were his best bet. So, he's gonna email you. Sounded super serious.*

Odd. Jasper was in a great mood every time Clark saw him, smiling and cheery. And always, always dressed so dapperly, in finely cut clothes that fit him like a second skin. He could have, at any point, looked the man up but that felt like breaking Jasper's privacy. Oh, for sure Clark had often imagined what the man did for a living, but he'd never asked and Jasper had never mentioned it. Instead, like any good patron/librarian transaction, they talked about books. Jasper's tastes were as varied as the wind in spring, and he was upfront with Clark about what he liked and what he didn't from previous recommendations.

Clark would never be able to admit that Jasper's visits were a highlight of his day. Hell, his week oftentimes.

From: Clark *Serious how?*

From: May *Involved/complicated kind of serious*

From: Clark *Color me intrigued*

From: May *Knew u would be*

His email to Jasper the next morning was all business, except for the final line where Clark asked if Jasper would be willing to try some dark sci-fi with a twist of horror. He had just finished this incredible debut book but it had seemed a tad too gory for Jasper's regular tastes.

Maybe the man would surprise him.

Clark had thrown the too-gory book idea in there as a way to hopefully save face if his email sounded too concerned. But the reply back was, in typical Jasper fashion, like a toothy grin on an emoticon-level of happy.

Hey there! I'm glad you got back to me. I am working on a project about the "ghost trails" that supposedly run across the state. Something to do with ley lines and the energy spilling out from them made certain places more susceptible to paranormal activity. I'm looking for anything - local history, archival info, journals, etc. And I can web browser search with the best of them, but May mentioned you'd done some archival work during your thesis -

Clark looked up from his screen and huffed. May was *certain* he and Jasper were *destined*. And while Clark might believe in ghosts and spirits and maybe even nebulous concepts like "The Veil", he did not believe that any entity like Destiny existed. And if it did, it certainly didn't care about some mid-thirties librarian in the upper Midwest and the mysterious, hot patron who seemed to favor him.

Clark went back to reading, drawn in by Jasper's words.

-and I would appreciate any tips you could give on searching for this info. She says you're the best at research, and I definitely believe it.

But I knew it already ;)

Anyways, I'll be by on Thursday. We HAVE to discuss this new series you got me started on! So good!

"Hey, May," Clark called out from his little office. He wasn't on desk duty until the afternoon, so he wanted to get more details from Jasper about this project. And there was no hiding it now - Jasper was about to find out how big of a ghost enthusiast he was. But Clark needed details; his brain screamed for them even as his heart pounded in his chest. It seemed unfair that a man that good looking was also a believer in the paranormal.

"Hey! Ooo!" May slunk into his office with a grin and a cup of coffee. "I know that smile. HG, right?"

"Yes and - "

May's brown eyes widened. "Yes and YES, my friend. Plus, you don't look bored, so it must be something really good."

"Bored?" Clark frowned, pushed up his glasses with a fingertip. "What's that supposed to mean?"

"You get this weird little stink face when you're bored," she said, snickering as Clark practically scoffed. "Anyways, you look like you found the key to the candy factory so..." She plopped down next to him, on the only other seating in his office; a rickety stool that should have long gone out to the trash. "Spill. I need to know."

Clark let May read over Jasper's email, but she got as far as "ghost trails" before punching a fist into the air. "Fuck yes!" May said.

"May!" Jasper's gaze darted to the hallway outside his office. His little nook was at the ass-end of the backroom that connected adult services to tech and cataloging, so traffic was a near-constant. Thankfully, no one was outside to hear May's cursing.

"Sorry, sorry." May hunched, leaning in to peer at his screen. "But oooh does he have you pegged."

Clark groaned and put his head into his hands. "Did you not realize what you were saying *when you said it*?" he hissed over May's snickers.

"Course I did."

"Of course you did," Clark groused while his friend chuckled. "Ugh. Okay, anyways. Can you read over my reply?"

"You bet." May rubbed her hands together, then held them out for Clark to pass over his laptop. "You just let me help you out here, lover boy. I bet we can have HG eating out of the palms of your hands -"

"May. Please. Professional."

"Professionally eating out of the palms of your hands." May grinned at Clark while he gave her the meanest gaze he could muster. "I'm kidding, I'm kidding."

Clark blew out a breath, torn between keeping his professionalism and letting May go wild on his reply. "Just help me out? Please? I don't want to make a fool of myself."

"I would never let you. Now..." May tilted her head to the side like a prize-fighter readying for a round. "On a zero to five eggplant emoji level, how enthusiastic do you want to sound coming out the gate?"

Chapter Three

"Oh, cool!"

"You think so?"

Sam grinned up at Bren. "Yeah! You know mushrooms can talk to each other? If they're in the same cluster, anyways."

"Huh, I did not. That's pretty neat, fry."

"Ugh," Sam moaned as only a nine-year-old could. "Mom should have never told you that nickname."

Bren shrugged, her expression as smooth as glass. "She's contractually obligated as far as I'm concerned."

Sam scrunched his nose up, making his freckles dance. "That sounds like made-up adult crap."

Bren widened her eyes to a dramatic level. "Pretty sure your mom would not want you saying crap."

"It's not a bad word."

Bren saw Sam's mom, a long-time greenhouse employee named Iris, pass by and grinned. "Let's ask!"

Against Sam's dramatic groaning, Bren called out Iris's name and a moment later, the woman appeared in the doorway. Teasing Sam was fun, especially because Bren had known the kid since he was two and had always been interested in plants and dirt and worms. A side effect of his mom overseeing the annual grow houses for certain, but Sam had an innate curiosity about the world. Apparently mushrooms were on the list now, too.

"This one says crap isn't a bad word," Bren said as Iris came into the small greenhouse.

Sam sighed and flopped down on a stool. "Mom..."

Iris barely stifled her laugh but winked at Bren. Everyone teased Sam; he was a "lifer", someone who had grown up at Pennyroyal & Mugwort, accompanying his mom from the time he could toddle. One of his first big words had been "chrysanthemum".

Sam grinned. "It's not on the list."

Bren raised a dark eyebrow and Iris chuckled again before saying, "The list of words he's not allowed to say quite yet. And you're right, turtle, so you can say crap- "

"Yes!"

"But once a day. Only."

"Aw." And then Sam wiggled his nose at Bren.

Bren bit the inside of her cheek to keep a straight face on. "How's the new crop of kale coming on?"

Iris nodded. "Pretty good, pretty good. I'm really wanting to see if the redbor kale comes in before starting another batch. It'll be really pretty if it sprouts."

"Good, thanks for keeping up on it."

Iris made finger guns at her, making Sam laugh. "You betcha, boss."

"And I thought you were the troublemaker," Bren groused to Sam, knowing she'd get another laugh.

"I gotta keep her in line!" Sam jumped down from his stool and started animatedly showing his mom the oyster mushroom farms Bren had started on earlier in the week. Bren smiled to herself, letting her mind wander as she refocused on her work.

It wasn't until Iris tapped her on the shoulder that Bren realized their chatting had stopped.

"Hey." Iris stared at her from behind her glasses, glittery purple frames glinting. "I'm only gonna ask once, and I wanted to wait to say something until Sam was out of earshot." Iris put a hand on Bren's arm, gave a brief squeeze, and let it drop. "Are you okay? You don't have to answer now. Text me later or something. But I know all this with restarting the mushrooms was probably kind of weird."

Bren thought for a moment, touched by Iris's caution. "A little weird, yeah. I'm glad Torrie was willing to see it through, but I wanted to get them started. It's past time to do it." Bren poked a finger into a soft, damp mound of dirt near her left elbow. "And working on these has given me some ideas for expansion."

Iris whistled softly. "You serious?"

Bren's smile was small but honest. "It's been on the business roadmap for a while but after everything that happened…"

"No, I get it." Iris gave the mushrooms a contemplative look before saying, "Well, I'm really proud of you. I've never loved my work before coming here and I know Sam looks up to you a ton. You've been good to us. All of us." Iris sniffed, then looked away. "Could I give you a hug?"

How could Bren not smile at that, not give in? "Of course."

For a long time, Bren had kept a firm line between boss and employee. But the crew that had helped her open Pennyroyal & Mugwort had worn her down. Maybe she had wanted it at times, their friendly smiles slowly turning into claps on the shoulder or high-fives. Even the occasional hugs. But the commercial, and Bren's act of heroism, going viral had changed a lot of things. It had certainly made Bren reevaluate *everything*. Made her question *everything*. And when the doubts crept in. Some of the worst nights had left Bren thinking she should shut the entire business down and live away from everyone and everything...and those high-fives, those hugs had brought her back from the brink.

Now, years after opening the greenhouse, Bren was willingly hugging someone she'd once only considered an employee, and now trusted as a friend.

"Well, okay, since we've both had enough feelings for one day, I'm going to find where my son ran off to." When Iris smiled like this, her nose wrinkled and Bren thought it was adorable.

"And I'll go see if Trey needs help with the mulch that just came in."

Iris gave Bren's braid a playful tug then ran off, leaving Bren and her mushrooms alone once more.

When Bren was halfway to the back lot where the mulch had been delivered, she decided to cut through one of the greenhouses. They usually had two or three open to customers this early in the season. The hardcore gardeners knew what they were doing and trusted that Pennyroyal & Mugwort did as well. She figured seeing a few familiar faces would be nice.

And she was right. Several of the people steering full carts of plants stopped their browsing to say hello. This was the kind of small talk Bren could handle. No inanity, no discussion of whether it might rain. She and these customers loved plants, loved gardening and tilling and the scent of fresh earth and new leaves. That love of growth and renewal - and the peace plants brought to her life - was why she'd reopened the greenhouse after her mother's death.

Clark chased ghosts. She grew plants. They each had their own ways of coping with loss.

"Oh my god!"

There was a hand on her arm, swiftly moving her back as a hanging plant fell to the ground. Cold water drenched her, sending rivulets of dirt down her face.

Staring up at her were a pair of wide eyes in a delicately-featured face, shock and worry registering as clear as day.

Bren blinked. One of the woman's eyes was a deep amber- hazel, the other a blueish green.

The water running down her face was bitterly cold, a welcome distraction despite the way it made her shiver. Bren swiped at it, sending droplets flying off her fingers. "What the hell just happened?"

"I am *so* sorry!" The person before Bren looked completely panicked. "I was reaching for that hanging plant and I didn't judge the height right and..." To the person's credit, they looked mortified. "I'm just glad it didn't hit you."

Bren realized a few people nearby had stopped and in the distance, she could see Trey and Iris headed her way; both of them with determined but worried expressions. But her immediate shock and anger at being nearly brained by a basket melted when she realized the culprit was truly upset. There was a fine tremble in the person's hands, visible only as they pushed a strand of bright pink hair out of their face.

Bren waved them off. "It's okay. Really. It's just water and dirt. If I didn't like those..." She gestured at the greenhouse.

"Right, of course." But the person was already pulling a small pack of tissues out of their purse. "I should have known better, or asked for help."

"Trust me, it's okay." Iris was now at her elbow and Bren took the cloth rags she offered. She was certainly smearing the dirt down her face, but it was also in her eyes and it stung to high heaven. After Bren mopped herself off a little, she gave the person a smile before turning to Trey. "I'm gonna go get cleaned up. Can you help this customer out, Trey?"

"Already there, Bren." Trey motioned the customer forward - out of the aisle - with a gentle hand and a crooked grin. "Now, did you want another basket like that one? I've got some nice ones in the back..."

"Just give them the basket," Bren muttered to Iris as they watched Trey and the customer walk off, the plant cart rattling over the concrete. "If someone's buying verbena this early, they hopefully know what they're doing."

"Got it. I'll fix it up, too, since these little guys lost a bit of dirt." Iris scooped up the hanging basket and trotted off after them.

Bren made quick work of the dirt after ducking into one of the staff bathrooms. She was wiping the final bits of it off her neck when her watch beeped with a text.

From: Iris *Hey, so that customer? Nice lady. Left you something at the checkout 2.*

From: Bren *Be there in a moment.*

Bren had to admit her curiosity was piqued. Given the woman's apologetic nature, it was probably just a note saying she was sorry. But when she reached checkout 2, Iris handed her a small blue envelope. In a swooping hand, the front bore the words, "To the woman I almost hit today".

Bren laughed softly as she traced the edge of the envelope with a finger. "Well, at least she's polite."

"Cute, too."

"Iris."

"What?" Iris shrugged. "I'm the picture of innocence."

"I think Sam is better behaved than you are." Bren rolled her eyes but she was smiling.

"That is...actually true, so I won't argue."

When Iris stepped back to give Bren some privacy, Bren opened the envelope and pulled out a small, folded piece of paper and a business card.

ELODIE WEAVER, PhD

RESEARCHER, FOLKLORIST, PLANT ENTHUSIAST
Professor at Alpine Hills University

weavere@alpinehills.edu

Baffled, Bren opened the slip of paper which was, she realized, the back of a flier from the corner market in downtown Wharton. She knew that market well and was there every week for basics like bread. In the summer, the market hosted a small farmer's stand. They sold the best tomatoes Bren had ever tasted, and she grew tomatoes year-round. That little connection between her and this overly apologetic stranger made something in Bren's chest flare as she read the note.

To Bren, the woman I dumped cold, dirty water on: I know you said not to apologize but I really am sorry. The perils of being a short person in a regular world is that sometimes I just reach for things and don't think about who is around. I should have asked for help, especially since the staff at Pennyroyal and Mugwort are always so nice.

I also wanted to say I LOVE your podcast and I can't wait for the new season in June! So this is the part where I offer my help, unbidden - but if you ever need the assistance of a folklorist, call me. There are so many fascinating myths around plants and I know you and Iris said you were interested in doing some historical stuff in the future. And...I've rambled enough.

And thanks so much for the free basket, you really didn't have to do that. I'll give it to my dad, he loves verbena.

At the bottom of the note was an arrow. Amused, Bren flipped the flier over, skimmed past some advertising for packs of meat on sale, and saw more handwriting.

Okay, I felt better writing this on a separate page, like you weren't pressed or pushed to read this if you didn't want to. But if you ever want to chat plants, or just...chat...

You seem nice and I wouldn't mind meeting new people. Why is it so hard to make friends as an adult? And why don't we try it more often? I'm game if you are.

Bren turned the card over in her fingers. Wondering.

Clark had been right. She did need to get out there. Maybe coffee with a new friend was a good step toward gearing herself up to another round of speed dating in a few weeks. And considering this *Elodie* had some similar interests. Even if things went wrong, Bren would get some coffee and plant talk out of it.

This is the part where Clark would tell me not to make a decision too hastily.

So what were her choices? She could always stay home and putter about the greenhouse, but she'd been doing that for years. She'd never leave if she kept this...horrible *pattern* up.

Bren got out her phone, smiling the entire time she typed out her message. Clark would be so proud of her when she told him over dinner about this. He would never expect his sister to text a stranger; someone who liked plants and dumped cold water on her head and yet was brazen enough to leave a note and business card.

Someone who had gorgeous eyes that lingered, even now, in Bren's memory.

> **To: Elodie** *Hey, it's Bren. From the greenhouse and the cold water. You're right, making friends as an adult is tough. I'm due for my early spring walk around the botanical gardens. Want to meet up, get coffee at the cart by the fountain?*

Bren tried to forget about the text, about the time that passed in that awful space between seeing "Read" and not getting a reply.

An hour or so later, she had one.

Clark really was going to wonder if she was a pod person at this point.

> **To: Bren** *Holy heck, hi! Oh, I wasn't expecting an answer at all. I DID dump dirty water on you. But okay yes I love the botanical gardens and that coffee cart! When are you free?*

Chapter Four

Clark tried to not think about Thursday and Jasper and the strange, swooping feeling in his belly when he pictured Jasper's face, but it was difficult. It made the days preceding drag on, with only his evening conversations with Bren to help him feel more grounded.

But last night's conversation over goulash had made Clark realize he was putting weight on something that could mean nothing. Every now and then his twin's staunch logic was a much-needed slap to the face, and he had no problem admitting when Bren was right.

"You're worrying too much," Bren said over a forkful of steaming pasta and beef. "So much that my food's going cold."

Clark sighed and put down his own fork to stare at his half-empty plate. "I mean, this is all just me doing my job, right? Jasper's a patron, I'm helping him with a research project." He then grinned at her. "And how am I responsible for your food going cold?"

"Uh huh." Bren didn't look convinced in the least but her tone was teasing. "And it's because I keep having to assuage your worries, Clark. You've got this." She reached over and put her hand on his. "You're a catch. If this hot patron can't see that, it's his loss."

Bren delivered the sentiment so matter-of-factly that Clark was left blinking in surprise. "Oh, okay then."

"Don't look so surprised." Bren waited until her next bite was gone before saying, "You've said before he's nice and clearly a ravenous reader. You two will probably get on like a house on fire."

"Nice and bookish?" He stabbed at his pasta, examined it before popping the forkful into his mouth. "I think I need more than that as a basis for dating."

Bren shrugged. "It's a start, right? You at least know something about him."

And as Clark opened his mouth to argue, he realized she was right. He and Jasper had already discussed favorite books, why certain tropes in genres did or didn't work, what they liked about this author or this series. It was work conversation, yes, but it had also given him some insights into the other man. Jasper liked detailed, flowing writing, the kind that let him into the minds of the characters. He loathed first-person point of view (something they agreed on), and loved it when stories dropped the reader into the action and slowly revealed the world over the course of the book.

Conclusion? Jasper was patient, had a good imagination, and was hungry for information. Maybe some of that was a stretch, but considering Clark had similar tastes, he didn't think he was too far off the mark. He did know some things about Jasper. But he was infinitely curious to learn more.

And now it was Thursday and here he was - at his desk in the back room, staring blindly at circulation reports for the biography section. Glancing to his right at the three books he'd pulled as recommendations for Jasper wasn't helping, either. So, it was either look at the wall, where the light blue paint was peeling from too many humid summers, stare at his inbox, or get up and shake it off. At least the third option would let him swing by the Coffee Depot on the main floor.

Maybe Jasper would let him buy them both coffee for their research session. Clark's hands grew clammy at the thought.

The image of him and Jasper in a small conference room, heads bent over a laptop, coffee cups close at hand, made Clark smile. Okay, it was a supremely geeky, deeply milquetoast fantasy, but it was *his*.

As he made his way toward the stairs, Clark ducked around two teenagers taking selfies in front of the stacks. That had been the thing recently, some kind of "stackie" or "shelfie" challenge on social media. So, there were a lot of teens and some younger kids running around the adult reference department after school. He didn't care one bit, since the library was meant for all and there was no rule saying older kids had to stay in their "designated" section. But he had to chuckle as he heard a regular patron, Mrs. Davidson, grumble about those same kids taking selfies. It was a grumble he'd gotten used to hearing over the last few weeks.

"Don't know why they're up here," Mrs. Davidson said as he passed by. "Clark, isn't there a teenager section in this building?"

"There is, Mrs. Davidson," Clark replied cheerily, stopping as a page wheeling a heavy book cart navigated around them. He was not going to let this woman dampen his spirits. "But who's to say they don't need John Steinbeck or Zora Neale Hurston for a class assignment? Or they just want to be up here? I'm not stopping you from going into the children's section for books for your grandkids."

The woman humphed, but he was proud at how she looked a little surprised at his cheek. "Well, but I'm an adult! I'm allowed down there."

"And they are allowed up here, as long as they abide by the rules. The ones we apply to all patrons."

Mrs. Davidson squinted at him through her thick glasses. "I've a mind to complain."

Clark picked up his pace again. "And I'm sure the folks at the desk can help." And he was off again, now thinking about getting tea instead of coffee as he descended the stairs to the ground floor.

Maybe it was Destiny or Fate or just some kind of karma he was owed. Seeing Jasper on the stairs, hair slicked back into a ponytail, raincoat dotted with moisture, wouldn't have happened if he'd been any more delayed. Jasper looked down at his phone as he climbed but the moment he looked up, Clark was only five steps above him.

Their gazes met.

Clark sucked in a breath.

Jasper smiled.

And Clark begged his mouth to get up to speed with his brain. He wanted to ask Jasper if he wanted any coffee or tea, or invite him to tag along while he ordered something for himself. Anything. Anything social, anything *normal* outside of talking about books in a professional capacity.

He could do this. He absolutely *could*. And not let the sudden maelstrom of butterflies in his stomach make him back down.

Clark gave what he hoped was a friendly smile. "Hey! I was just heading to the Depot for some tea. Do you want anything?"

Jasper's smile grew. The butterflies quadrupled. "You read my mind," Jasper replied as he motioned Clark down the stairs. "That rain is freezing. I was going to come up and get situated, then go back down, but this works just fine."

"Oh, good!" Clark mentally face palmed. Gods, he sounded like an overeager puppy. But Jasper just kept grinning.

The Coffee Depot sat between the media department and the study rooms, tucked into a nook that had once hosted the patron hold shelves, where folks could pick up their requested titles. A few years ago, the library was remodeled and a coffee shop was one of the biggest requests from the community (and the staff). On a day like today, the shop was doing a ton of business, so Clark and Jasper joined the queue.

It was truly unfair, Clark thought as he looked over the man's aquiline profile, how beautiful some people were. Even though they were twins, Bren had a no-nonsense energy about her; in the way she stood tall and proud, how accurately she used her radar for bullshit, and even down to the blunt edges of her bangs. Clark always felt messy, sometimes even unrefined, around her.

He was the portrait of a slightly forgetful professor, one boyfriend had said. Granted, it was said with fondness but it had made Clark feel small. Just because he fit the stereotype of nerdy librarian with cardigans and glasses didn't mean he had a one-note personality.

Clark wanted to shake all that off, so after a few moments of silence, he said, "So this project. The ghost trails?"

Immediately, Jasper lit up like the sun. *Truly unfair*, Clark thought, even as he smiled at the man's enthusiasm. "Yes, so I know it's rather obscure. Which is why I'm asking for your help." Jasper lowered his voice as more people lined up behind them and the queue moved forward. "I'm writing a book about the folklore of the state and the ghost trails have always fascinated me. I want to make it at least a chapter in the book, but I'm stalling on my research. There aren't any papers written on it. I started to think I made it all up, and then when I went on a ghost hunt last fall, everyone I talked to had stories about it."

Clark's head buzzed with all this new information.

Jasper liked things about the paranormal.

He maybe believed in ghosts, or at least mulled the possibility of their existence.

Jasper had been on ghost hunts.

"Holy shit," Clark breathed out, his mouth far ahead of his usual stringent filter.

"What?" They moved up in line again but Jasper was staring at him.

"I uh.... sorry." Clark swallowed hard, pretended to glance at the electronic menu board above the Depot's counter. But his grin wouldn't be stopped and the urge to mess with the curls on top of his head took over, so Clark shoved his hands in his pockets. Any time Bren saw him twirling his hair, she would gently remove his fingers. It had always been a nervous habit, but after their parents died, he'd taken to touching it so much that he'd developed dermatitis on his scalp. So, when it reared up on occasion, Clark would tuck his hands away. "What I meant was I'm kind of amazed. Which hunt was it? Detroit? Marquette? There's only a few during autumn, with the way it can snow so early."

As Jasper's brows drew down, a little nick formed between them. He had nice eyebrows, Clark mused as he watched understanding blossom over the other man's face, slowly morphing his confusion into a bright smile. Nice, thick eyebrows slightly darker than his honey-brown hair. They made Jasper's green eyes stand out. "Wait, you ghost hunt?" Jasper asked delightedly.

"Have since I was about sixteen, but I started going to the organized ones after college." Clark shrugged. "Poor college student, you know."

"Absolutely. I have to say, finding out my favorite librarian is a fellow ghost hunter is simply fantastic." Jasper clapped his hands, then rubbed them together. The sharp sound rang out through the tall, open atria behind them; a few people turned to look but Jasper was oblivious. And he was very, very cute when he grinned.

Clark tensed his hands in his pockets, slowly balling them up. *Favorite librarian.* That made him feel warm all over. Like a teenage crush mixed in with the understanding of adulthood, and topped with the glow that only came when you met another person who liked the same things you did. That was a special affirmation, a unique connection.

"And it was Marquette, the hunt I went to." Jasper leaned in, the secret hush of his words tumbling into Clark's ear and shooting lightning down his spine. "It snowed. It was *so* bloody cold."

Jasper said *bloody* like a purr, a rumbling thing that had Clark sucking in a breath. His fists balled up tighter. "Sounds awful."

"It was. Very."

They stepped up to the counter as Otto, the depot manager for the afternoons, waved to them. "Clark! Hey, man. Want the usuhz?"

"Uh, no, and hey, Otto. Can I get a chai latte, and whatever Jasper wants."

"I do want the usuhz, Otto." Jasper gave Clark a look. "I come here a lot, usually stop on my way out."

"He really does. And I'll have those right up!" Otto raced off to the other side of the counter where jars of coffee beans sat on display, and one of his staff stepped up to take their payment.

"Let me." Jasper reached over Clark and handed the clerk his credit card. "Consider it a thank you for your help."

Clark laughed, the sound weak. Oh, he most certainly had a crush. It was solidified with Jasper's sweet gesture. A few patrons had bought him coffee before, but none of them had been Jasper. Looking like he did. *Handsome son of a bitch.* "Guess it's a good thing it's only a few dollars, otherwise I'd have to go check the staff policy on accepting gifts."

"You should get gifts. Gestures of gratitude from the people you help." Jasper motioned in an arc to his left, toward the stairs leading to Clark's department. "You librarians do important work. And I know part of your typical day doesn't entail helping strangers with their wild research needs."

"One, thank you." They took the cups Otto handed them, then Jasper followed Clark not up the stairs, but toward the back of the building where the small conference rooms were. "Two, my job description covers pretty much anything and everything patrons ask. Local folklore is not even close to the stranger things I've been asked for."

"Color me intrigued."

"Ha, it had to do with the history of fountain pens and morphed into a months-long project on how a particular red dye was made and it became the color of a small kingdom in middle Europe. It was fascinating, but very niche."

Jasper was silent for a long moment while they reached the door to the conference room and Clark unlocked it. "I'm afraid to ask what the *weirdest* thing you've been asked for is," Jasper finally said.

Once settled at the table so they could face the windows, Clark realized how close Jasper was. Clark was already reeling from what he'd learned about Jasper, but their knees brushed and his mind shorted out for a moment.

Clark cleared his throat to give himself some space before speaking. "So ah, to start, I think we should pull some historical accounts from around the time the ghost trail stories started up. I've read some of them before." Clark took a few minutes to navigate through the scans of diaries from the late 1600s and early 1700s. They both leaned in at the same time to examine Clark's laptop screen. "When the French first settled in Michigan, they were already a pretty spirited bunch, even with the cold winters. These are diaries from settlers at that time and as you can see, there were a lot of sightings."

"Incredible," Jasper breathed. Clark felt the air shift, felt that breath on his neck. He bit down on a shiver. "How did you access this? I thought it was only Alpine College that had these scans in their archives."

"The library partnered with Alpine several years ago, when database costs started going through the roof. They pay some, we pay the rest, and everyone with a library card or an Alpine student or staff ID can use the databases. And..." Clark opened the next tab. "That includes the archives at the college. We advertise the access, but admittedly there's an information saturation point and library databases aren't high on the list for ninety-nine percent of folks. But when you need it, it's super handy." He was quietly pleased with how in awe Jasper seemed of the entire thing, and Clark had to remember that most folks didn't think about their library, or the nature of information gatekeeping. Jasper's raw enthusiasm was like getting extra sprinkles on his ice cream.

"Can we keep going?" Jasper asked as he pulled out a notebook and pen. "This is amazing."

"Yeah, of course."

Together, they sipped their drinks and examined several diary entries about "migrating ghosts" and other spectral sightings settlers documented, with Jasper taking rapid notes in a shorthand Clark couldn't read. As the room's printer churned out copy after copy of those worn pages, Clark worked up the nerve to ask what had been sitting on his tongue. "So, ghost hunting...if it's okay to ask, what got you started? Most folks who do it have a story. And it's okay if you don't want to share."

Jasper gave him a small smile before tapping the end of his pen on his chin as his gaze went distant. "I used to see things," he replied quietly, not meeting Clark's gaze. "When I was a kid. It made my parents think there was something wrong with me, but my brother always believed me. And when I got older, I became more curious about the things I'd experienced. Lights, voices, chills in the middle of summer. My brother thought I was sensitive to...I'm not sure, energies, perhaps. And when I got older, I started reading everything I could get my hands on. I stopped seeing things when I was about fourteen, but I think I've always believed. I think the world's too big, too unknown still, for there to not be a little mystery still."

Jasper tugged at his caramel-colored turtleneck with a shy smile. "Suffice to say, even now, I still find myself wondering if I'll ever feel something again. See something, maybe. It makes me wonder if becoming an adult leaves those more...open parts of us lost to the days of childhood. But I never stopped believing, and I don't think I ever will."

The intense, vibrant *honesty* in Jasper's voice struck a chord deep in Clark. It almost *hurt* to hear someone speak like that; so much that Clark had to blink away the tears that had suddenly formed. If Jasper noticed, he kindly said nothing and instead reached for his cup.

The back of his hand brushed over Clark's.

Clark wasn't the kind to feel faint at such a casual, accidental touch. And yet...

Finally, Clark managed to say, "I get it. I do. The mystery and the personal connections to what might be something more." Clark gestured at the computer screen. "And it's nice to realize we're not the only ones who know there's something out there."

Jasper's voice took on a dreamy quality that thickened his accent. It was terribly cliche, but Clark wanted the man to simply *talk* to him in that rolling, lilting thing that brought forth images of green hills and vast blue sky. "Voices from history reaching out even now, telling their stories. Giving comfort. Letting us know we're not alone in the dark."

Without meaning to, Clark sighed. Jasper's gaze narrowed in on him and Clark felt it like a touch. A purposeful one this time, and it made Clark's cheeks heat. "Sorry," Clark said, quickly leaning back.

"Don't apologize." Jasper tapped his bottom lip with a finger. Clark's eyes got stuck on that damn treble clef tattoo. "I have to admit, I'm not surprised."

"Surprised?" God, did his voice just *squeak*?

Jasper's tapping stopped, but his gaze grew warm and heavy. "I knew you were good at your job, Clark. But it's clear you're passionate. Passion is a good thing, a rare trait."

Clark's voice - and possibly his common sense - fled for several long seconds that felt like hours. He needed to save face, and fast. "So, ghost trails? There are a few mentions in the early 1700s but they don't really pick up steam until around 1760, when there were skirmishes between white settlers and the indigenous tribes living in the Upper Peninsula."

The spell broke. Jasper leaned back as well but instead of straightening in his chair, he crossed his legs and laid his notebook in his lap. "Can you show me how to recreate this search? I'd love to be able to do it at home."

Clark almost said *no* before he realized that would be against his job duties and his very nature. He simply didn't want Jasper to stop coming to see him. "Yeah, sure."

After another hour, Clark was torn. He was smitten with the way Jasper talked, the way he used his hands when making a particular point. And Jasper had told him about seeing ghost trails, little bits of light like will-o'-wisps. But instead of the ghost trails leading a brave adventurer to their doom, ghost hunters had seen them talked about following them like a journey, one usually ending in the ghost hunter experiencing something unforgettable.

When Clark asked about Jasper's ghost trail experience, the man smiled mysteriously, then winked. "A story for another time, I think. I should be heading back home. Work never waits, I'm afraid."

"Yes, of course." Clark paused. "What is it you do? If you don't mind - "

"I never mind. Not from you."

Clark had been fighting with himself all afternoon. One moment, Jasper was all business, entirely focused on following Clark's instructions on how to search the various archive databases. The next, he'd be coy; quieter, voice deeper but with an unmistakable warmth. Flirty, even.

Or maybe Clark was just so hard up for romantic company that he was turning a regular instruction session into something more. God, did Bren ever feel this out of depth with people? She always seemed so sure of herself and it often drove Clark up a wall. And here he was feeling flustered by a nice voice and a set of finely boned hands.

"That's uh..." Clark swallowed hard. There was no judgment on Jasper's face. Only a simmering intensity that twisted something up inside him. "Right, well."

Jasper chuckled. "I'm a musician. Classical, mostly. Violin, piano, cello. But I do some freelance things with guitar and drums."

Clark was *doomed*. Handsome and supremely talented. Shit. "Okay, wow. I'm extremely impressed."

Jasper had the consideration to look embarrassed. "Please don't be. It's a living, an honest one, but not nearly as glamorous as the movies make it appear. I mostly putter around my condo in slippers, wearing headphones as if they're permanently attached to my head. I do independent music lessons as well, when I have the time."

Clark definitely wasn't seeing an issue with that image. He pictured Jasper in some patterned robe and sheepskin-lined slippers, gorgeous hands waving in the air as if conducting. So, he gestured at himself and said, "And I'm a cardigan-wearing librarian. Lean into the stereotypes, my friend. They give us power."

Jasper let out a snort. "The power to impress others with our ability to be what they expect?"

"And then go on to shatter those implications and expectations." Clark gestured between them. "Ghost hunters come in all forms. Sometimes they're just simple librarians and their inquisitive, quick-learning patrons."

"So, which am I? Just a patron, or a friend?"

The idea that had been simmering in the back of Clark's mind came roaring into the forefront, eager to be let loose. *Take the shot,* he could almost hear Bren say.

"Well, if we're friends, then I have a duty to inform you that there's a hunt going on in a few weeks up in Haven. And uh, as a friend..." Clark bit his lip. "As a friend, I should inform you that there are still tickets available and Haven has the second-highest number of reportings in the state. It was several different towns over the last few centuries, all basically built on top of each other. Plus, it's near the site of a pretty tragic story. Ripe hunting ground."

Jasper's stare bore into him. Seconds passed. When Clark couldn't hardly stand it anymore, Jasper said softly, "You are a very kind, thoughtful person. Inviting me to an event you clearly are excited for, when you don't even know me."

But I do, Clark wanted to argue. *I do because I've seen things, too, and you speak about the supernatural in the same way I feel about it and you don't demonize or glamorize it. You know it's a tool. A connection. A cord that ties and binds us all together. A shared memory, across untold shared experiences.*

"Could I have your number?" Jasper asked, breaking the spell as they stared at each other. Inches apart. *So close.* "I would love more details on this hunt. Maybe we could plan a bit together."

"I'd like that."

"Good." Jasper's smile promised things Clark didn't dare linger on. What had been subtle was now making him twitch. And Jasper looking like the cat with the canary wasn't helping. "I hope it won't come across too eager if I text you tonight."

But Clark was already ahead of him, pulling out his phone and adding Jasper's number. The text he fired off simply read "Haven MI" and linked Jasper to the event site. "Can't be eager if you're second in line," he teased.

"So you're the eager one?"

This was flirting. Definitely flirting. Clark felt sweat run down his back but the little voice in his head egging him on kept saying *more more more*. "I think that depends."

One dark blond eyebrow arched. Questioning. Daring. "Oh?"

Now or never. "If you'll let me buy you a drink while we plan."

Jasper's smile didn't deflate as he said, "As long as you aren't bothered by sobriety."

"No, not at all. I'm not a big alcohol fan to begin with." Clark flushed and turned away. "Sorry, the whole *go out for a drink* thing was a cheesy line and I should have thought about my word choice. But what about meeting at the Golden Unicorn Cafe? It's on the west side, but if that's too far, there are a few nice coffee houses near downtown, too."

"I'm on the west side, and I love the Golden Unicorn." Jasper picked up his phone and typed, fingers flying over the screen.

Clark's phone buzzed.

> **From: Jasper** *It's nice to get the chance to know you better, Clark. My favorite librarian.*

Long after Jasper left, Clark caught himself smiling. It did not go unnoticed, but mercifully May let him have his little secret. When he arrived at home that night, Clark went through his normal routine of decompressing with some cycling, then dinner, tea, and finally settling in bed with his book. Only then did he allow himself to write Jasper an email, detailing his usual set-up for ghost hunts and proposing they combine knowledge to do some hunting together.

Clark read the email twice. It was only after that second pass he realized how bad the sentence, "Maybe we should pitch our tents next to each other" sounded.

He kept it in anyway.

He also sent along some pages from the first book he'd found that mentioned ghost trails. It would have been so easy to send everything - all the podcasts, videos, and blogs citing experiences with the paranormal; academic papers discussing the power of belief and how human interpret nebulous concepts like the soul and the afterlife; and even a list of favorite reads on anything to do with ghosts, specters, apparitions, and the like. He could have sent it all...and immediately driven Jasper away by being *too* eager.

Instead, he left it open-ended. An invitation for Jasper to trade information and resources with him. To share in their hobby, their passion. Jasper was interesting and friendly, but Clark wanted to know what made him tick. Few things were more personal than someone's experiences. He finished out the email with a few times and days for their coffee meet-up.

Satisfied, Clark went to bed trying to remember the last time he'd been this excited.

Chapter Five

It was just one of those days, apparently.

"Shit," Bren muttered as she inspected the broken switch on the electric kettle in the staff room at the greenhouse. She had a kettle back at home and it would only take her the ten-minute walk through the woods to fetch it. One of the many nice things about living on the same property as your business was convenience. But on a day like this one, where several small things had gone wrong, she'd really needed that cup of tea. So, she was sure as fuck going to walk over to the house, make an entire thermos of tea, and bring it back.

Or she was, until Iris radioed her. "Hey boss, you might want to lay low."

Bren snatched the radio out of its holster on her belt. "Oh, that is not what I wanted to hear just now."

"I'm sorry. But there's a...Jesus, did they come in a *bus*?"

Something sank into the pit of Bren's stomach. "Please don't tell me."

"I uh...wait, hold on. Terry's got them right now."

The radio went dead. Bren stared at it hard. Waiting. She did not like where this was going. It was either a bus full of people pulling up an hour before they closed shop for the day, or...

"Bren, stay where you are."

"Iris."

"They're looking for the 'mushroom wall hero'. Some kind of...fuck, I'm not sure, some kind of documentary project thing. Talking to local heroes wherever they go."

Well, that was a big nope. Bren's heart started to race but her hand on the radio didn't shake. She could be proud of that later, when she drank a bunch of whisky and fell into bed. "I'm in the break room. Iris, how many of them are there?"

"Five," came Iris's immediate reply. "Camera, sound, interview dude with a weird haircut, and two...I don't honestly know who they are. They pulled up in some kind of big camper thing. Just stay put, we've got this."

Bren sank into a chair. "Thanks," she said, hating how small her voice was. "Let me know when they're gone? Or at least when I can sneak over to the house?"

"Of course."

The radio fell silent again and Bren found herself immediately missing Iris's voice. She would never feel more alone than those months after she'd saved one of her employees from being crushed. The entire thing had been some insane chain of events.

Of course it had to happen on the day they were filming a new commercial for Pennyroyal & Mugwort.

Of course Bren had caught sight of the movers losing control of the cart on which the new mushroom wall supplies sat.

And of course the cameras had been rolling as she tackled poor Ginny out of the way as the incredibly heavy concrete and wood wall slabs toppled to the ground.

The uncut version of the commercial had gone viral, Bren was labeled a hero, and suddenly, in that very weird way the Internet worked, she had invites from local to national talk shows, podcasts, and even interview requests from big names. Everyone had wanted to talk to the "mushroom wall hero" (among other monikers complete strangers had bestowed her with). Bren had turned them all down, and had made sure that any donations had gone to Ginny and their family. Ginny had escaped with minor cuts and bruises and a fractured wrist. The doctor had said the concrete would have crushed them if Bren hadn't been there.

Bren had wanted *nothing* to do with the spotlight even as a kid. As an adult, the mere thought of her face on some TV news channel or plastered across a digital newspaper made her want to hide and never, ever come out again. It was more than aversion; it was fear.

Bren had long ago learned that fear sometimes didn't need a reason. It would simply be there, waiting. The fear had sent her anxiety and depression into a vicious cycle. But fear of being recognized had then turned into fear of leaving her bed, fear of losing the family business and somehow disappointing Mom.

It had been a very dark hole out of which she'd dug herself. And it hadn't been easy. But even now, almost eighteen months later, Bren could still feel the vomit crawling up her throat, the heavy thump of her heart, the roaring in her ears. The anxiety had sent her into a spiral and only now had she been able to find level footing again. She'd already been psyching herself out for the coffee meet-up with Elodie tomorrow. And now this.

Bren felt sick.

Time crawled as she waited for the radio to buzz or her phone to go off. Eventually, Bren gave in and rested her forehead on her arm and closed her eyes. If she breathed slowly, steadily, as her therapist had shown her, she would feel better. Bren had scoffed at that notion when Dr. Martin had suggested it, but he had been correct. She was a shallow breather, something that only got worse when she freaked out.

"You'll hyperventilate yourself into a blackout," he'd said more than a few times with genuine concern in his eyes. Dr. Martin was affable and good-natured, a man in his late sixties who wore the wisdom of his years on his face and in his thinning white hair. Bren had liked him instantly.

"Hey, Bren. Are you still there?"

Bren jolted upright and fumbled for the radio, the black plastic case slipping against her sweaty hands. "Yeah."

"You're clear. I don't think the director or whoever I talked to bought it, but I told her you were off property and Ginny had the day off."

"Oh, thank fuck. Where did Ginny duck into?"

Iris giggled. "She pulled a video game hero move and jumped into the back of Terry's truck and pulled a tarp over herself."

Bren laughed but it was a bitter, small sound. "Fucking hell. That's so ridiculous. Look at us, hiding away from cameras because of..." She sighed and cradled her head in her free hand. "I wish people would move on."

"I know you do. One day at a time, Brenna."

"Ouch, using the full name, huh?"

"It's my Mom-mode cred."

"How does that work with your kid? His name is just *Sam*."

"That's what middle names are for. Now go, before they change their minds and come back."

On her walk back home, Bren pondered the same line of thinking she always did when that damn video reared its ugly head. She would, of course, do it all over again to make sure Ginny was safe. But the upheaval it had caused in her and Clark's life, for the greenhouse and everyone who worked there? Never, ever worth it. Maybe they were all a bunch of strange loners who preferred plants to people, but the staff at the greenhouse had all taken their cues from Bren on avoiding publicity. Ginny had given one interview to a local news channel and had spent almost the entire time praising Bren and gloating about how great the greenhouse was to work at.

But that video had also shown her the darker, uglier parts of herself that Bren had always felt she'd had to hide. Her snappish realism, even pessimism; her tendency to bite off more than she could chew; her impatience. And worst of all, how she would withdraw when she was feeling the bottomless pit of depression. It had always been like this, even since she was young and would spend hours after school and on weekends staring at the ceiling, feeling no motivation or desire to do anything at all. The new drugs and talk therapies over the years helped. The greenhouse helped. Clark helped.

She didn't want to disappoint any of them ever again.

Bren watched a cardinal take off from a nearby branch, the red flash of its wings intense against the almost-black trees. Spring was nearly here, which meant the busy season was already ramping up. Her work would sustain her, keep her hands and mind occupied. And thinking of anything else outside her obligations felt too big, too overwhelming.

She remembered her coffee meet-up tomorrow and sighed. She'd go, but it would take some effort to not bow out at the last minute. That wouldn't be fair to Elodie, or to herself really. Forcing herself to do things when the depression settled in sometimes led to good things. And she could really use a good thing right now.

The conservatory grounds were a popular spot when the weather hinted at warmth, so Bren immediately veered off the main paths. The grounds were huge, spanning hundreds of acres of both well-maintained gardens and overgrown woods, with paths for almost any ability level strewn across like a haphazard neighborhood. It would have been better on a grid, but Bren knew the place's history; added to over decades, as land was donated or purchased by the wealthy and influential. Despite all that, it was a nice spot for a long stroll, which was what Bren needed to clear her head.

Yesterday's panic rolled around in her mind all day, so much that Iris had moved her off loading dock duty with a gentle shove when Bren had, at one point, stared off into space. And Iris knew that Bren would never want to get in anyone else's way at the greenhouse. "You're the epitome of a good boss," Iris had said when she'd put Bren in the herb tents. "So breathe in some rosemary and worry about that lavender that looks a little wimpy. We're good on the loading dock."

The message, loud and clear? "Boss, you're in the way and we want to get this hard stuff done, but we don't want to insult you or make you think we don't know what's up. We've got this, don't worry." But said with a kind smile and the gentle eyes of one of her most trusted employees. And her friend.

Now, as the sun warmed the concrete under her feet, causing several puddles of snow to melt and drip down the stairs to one of the center courtyards, Bren took a moment. This was her favorite spot in the gardens, this wide-open expanse of concrete walkways around a massive fountain. The fountain's angelic figure had long faded to jade green from its original copper. But the hemline of the angel's long dress and its sandaled feet were worn down even more, rubbed by thousands of luck-wishers over the decades. On the left side of the fountain's square base, a young couple posed while their photo was snapped. To the right, Lady's Coffee Cart steadily churned through a line of customers hoping for hot drinks to ward off the bite in the air.

Bren scanned the line of customers, looking for pink hair and the bright teal fleece Elodie had mentioned in her follow-up email. The woman's words had been kind but excited, leaving Bren to feel a flicker of excitement as well.

"So, wait." Clark's grin at her this morning, a telling one over the rim of his coffee cup, had been gently teasing. *"You're meeting up with someone for coffee. You're meeting up with the person who dumped cold, dirty water on you, who also is a researcher at the university. The same university you went to for agriculture and business studies."* His dark eyes were wide behind his glasses, making her brother look ten years younger, even if he was wearing a patterned burgundy housecoat that belonged in a smoker's den from the 1960s. *"It's fate, Bren. Gotta be. And now you might not have to go to speed dating at Flannery's."*

Bren had scoffed at him over her own cup of coffee. *"This is just...meeting someone new."*

"Otherwise called a date."

"It's not a date, Clark." Her tone snapped when she didn't mean to and instantly she backpedaled. *"Sorry. Yesterday with the documentary crew thing fucked up my head but that's no excuse."* She left her seat to walk over and throw an arm around his shoulders. *"Sorry."*

"I know. It's okay."

"It's not."

The smile he gave her had been small, but honest. *"You're my sister. If we don't get churlish with each other every now and then, it wouldn't be right."*

Bren sighed. Oh, Clark. Heart of gold under all that messy dark hair and deeply questionable fashion sense. And after how open he'd been with her about his interactions with Hot Glasses of late, she really needed to not snap to defense all the time.

Bren went back to watching the line at the coffee cart and...well, wouldn't you know it? She spotted a bright teal fleece jacket hustle into view. Elodie looked like a colorful songbird amongst all the black, brown, and navy jackets migrating around the fountain and court-yard. Bren's hands were cold and her mind felt full of broken glass, but that little sight made things feel better.

She took the stairs and got to the fountain before Elodie turned and looked right past her. Then looked back. Noticed her. And grinned so brightly it almost hurt Bren's eyes. "Hey! Oh, hey, you made it!" Elodie rushed over but stopped short by a few feet. "I figured I'd be early and could just take in the sunshine for a moment, but you're here."

There was no disappointment in her tone. Elodie looked and sounded genuinely happy to see Bren. The warm glow in Bren's chest was...*new.* "Hey, yeah. Nice to see you. Thanks for braving the cold to do this."

"I actually like the cold." Elodie laughed. "I know, weird, but I go out into the woods a lot when it's chilly or even snowing. I do photography as a hobby and there's just nothing quite like the quiet of a winter morning." She gestured to the trees around them. "Or when things start to go green, just at the edge of spring."

"I get it."

"I figured if anyone did, it would be you. Surrounded by beautiful plants all day." Elodie sighed, the sound gusty. "So, I uh..." Strangely, Elodie flushed and turned away, her gaze darting to the ground, but her words tumbled out at a clip. "So, you probably don't remember me from this, but we met about a year ago. I had just moved to Jackson Park to take a job at the university and my little flat was so lifeless. So, I found Pennyroyal & Mugwort online and stopped in. You helped me find a few easy-care ferns and you were just so nice and I...always remembered that. One of my first interactions in town with someone kind who actually seemed to care."

"Oh." Bren thought back, trying to clear the fog from her memories around that time. She'd been neck-deep in a bout of depression then, so things were a tad murky. As they joined the line for the coffee cart, Bren wracked her brain.

Pink hair. No...purple? Something flickered in the corners of her mind. *Passing over a fern to a set of hands, her gaze catching on the bright enamel bangles that clinked when the other person moved.*

"Did you have purple hair? In a braid? And a lot of bracelets on?

Elodie's mouth dropped open. "You do remember! Okay, I'm a little excited, gotta admit." She scuffed at a pebble with the toe of her boots. "You were kind, and I was constantly tripping over my words, but you helped me. And I went back to the greenhouse a few times, trying to..." Elodie yanked her gaze back up but now she held steady. "I kept trying to work up the nerve to offer my help. I'm a folklorist by trade, so I track how stories and culture intertwine. And my recent project is plant folklore. I'd love to put all of that to some use outside of academic papers that get put behind paywalls. And I think the greenhouse's podcast would be a good avenue for something like that. I can provide research or find stories you'd be interested in. There are tons of botanical drawings available online, and I've even looked into those artists, some of whom are completely fascinating."

After all of that, Elodie smiled and held her arms out as if to say, "So what now?"

Bren was a little stunned. It was a great idea, actually. She and Iris had discussed finding the time to do a proper research project. Elodie definitely had the passion and knowledge to assist. If that meant she and Elodie got more time together, to get to know each other, then that was a nice bonus.

"I'll have to talk to Iris, of course," Bren said slowly.

"Oh gosh, of course!"

"And we can make you a part-time employee of the greenhouse. A little extra cash–"

"No, Bren, I don't want any money."

All her fuzzy feelings ground to a halt. "No, we would have to pay you. Not only for the sake of what's right by you, but for legal reasons."

Elodie's smile was gone, replaced by a frown. Bren wanted her to smile again. "So, I can't help, as a friend?"

Bren shook her head. "A one-time favor is one thing. But week after week? No, we'd need to make you a research assistant."

There was something canny and clever lurking behind the blue and green and muted brown of Elodie's eyes. If Bren got through this meet-up without blurting out, *I think your eyes are gorgeous*, she'd count herself very lucky. "Hmm, okay, I didn't think this through too well. What if I take what you pay me and spend it all on plants?"

Bren smirked at her. "That's your prerogative. And you wouldn't be the only employee to do that. There's a good discount."

Elodie gaped at her for a fraction of a second, then chuckled. The sound rolled into a full-bodied laugh. "Oh, you're funny. I like that."

A simple statement, right? Bren thought as they stepped up and placed their orders. *I like that*. Friendly, kind, a nod to perhaps a shared sense of humor. But for reasons that eluded her, that little statement also made her feel light, almost fizzy.

Maybe *this* was what it was like to meet new people. To make a new friend. And of course if Iris or Clark were here, they'd smile knowingly and remark how Elodie was exactly Bren's type. It was sometimes difficult being a tall, broad woman in a world that still clung to outdated ideas of femininity, and Bren's taste running to shorter, more petite people could fill bucket after bucket of stereotypes.

"Well, I don't know about funny," Bren replied as she nodded her thanks to the older woman passing over their drinks. "But I would like to know more about how you got into this kind of research." She sipped the scalding hot coffee. It was perfect - near boiling, black with two sugars.

"Yes, of course." Elodie sipped her own drink as they started to walk down one of the main paths. Bren couldn't help but watch as Elodie licked away whipped cream from her cup lid. "I will try very hard not to get into the weeds too much, but once you open the floodgates..."

"No worries. I know what that's like." Bren gestured to herself. "Plant lady extraordinaire here. Though I get teased for not having anything but ferns in my place."

Elodie lit up. "I love ferns! They're so fascinating. Depending on the culture or civilization or religion, they could symbolize good luck, longevity, new love. Plus, they're absolutely beautiful."

"I agree. They were the first plant I ever grew in abundance. I credit them as to why I re-opened the greenhouse."

"Re-opened?" Elodie froze with a guilty look. "Sorry, I shouldn't pry."

Bren pointed toward a bench and at Elodie's nod, they both sat. The bench was big enough for the two of them, but bundled up as they were, their coats and knees wound up touching. Elodie didn't seem to mind.

"It's not prying. I like telling the story now. It's kind of..." Bren sucked in a deep breath. "It's nice to get to talk about it now. So, the greenhouse, which I reopened after my mom died, was more of a hobby for her. She mostly sold to people in town and would go to farmer's markets. There was always something stopping her from making it into a full business." Bren shrugged, took another sip. "After she was gone, I figured the best way for me to memorialize her was to make her dream a reality. Plus, I'd get to put my agricultural knowledge to good use."

Elodie hummed softly. There was a tiny smile gracing the corners of her mouth. Bren felt no pressure or expectation from that look, only simple interest. "That's incredibly sweet. I bet your mom would have loved everything you've done with the greenhouse. It's a soothing place to visit." She shot Bren a little smile. "Even if my wallet suffers every time I go there."

Bren returned the smile, feeling warmth blossom in her chest. "How many ferns have you bought?"

"So many. I have five at home, two at my office, and I've given them as gifts to everyone I know at this point." Her smile turned into a grin. "Like I said, murder on my wallet but so worth it."

Bren turned on the bench so she could better face Elodie. Curiosity rose in her as she realized how easy it was to talk to this stranger. It felt natural, simple in a way Bren hadn't experienced in a long time. Not since she'd met Iris, in fact.

This was good for her. For her mental health, yes, but also in that quiet, lingering way Bren knew her depression latched onto. Left to her own devices for too long, she would fixate on one thing and run it into the ground. Having someone new to talk to, someone who didn't press or pry, but *listened*? It made Bren want to crack open her sternum and watch all the darkness, the grief, the loneliness pour out so she could be whole again, clean again.

"I'm not trying to change the subject just because," she said as Elodie maneuvered to face her as well. "But I really do want to know more about your work. And we can talk about how it might fold into the podcast, but I'm just curious."

"I'm flattered."

Sincerity bled into Elodie's tone. Bren wanted to return the favor, to listen and observe and make this new person in her life feel heard. She leaned back, propped her arm on the top of the bench, and said, "Flattery or not, I'd love to hear about it."

Chapter Six

The Golden Unicorn was packed with color - the walls, floors, counters, tables, shelves. All of it clashing and clanging about on the senses. And somehow, it worked.

Hot pink walls, dark blue floors, gleaming white counters that had gold glitter embedded in them, and decorations ranging from cute unicorn plushies in every shade of the rainbow to creepy, wide-eyed dolls. It was a strange, but very fun, place and they had the best coffee in the city, in Clark's opinion.

He was very early. *Very*. But having a cup of coffee before Jasper arrived was what he needed, and getting to the cafe between busy hours meant he had his choice of booths, so Clark picked one that faced the door. It was tucked into a corner and partially hidden behind a column decorated with glittering fairy lights and stickers from businesses around town. His coffee had come in a wide, squat cup decorated with haphazard red and yellow polka dots, and it was steaming so much his glasses fogged up on the first sip. Clark took them off, set them aside, and tried not to glance at his backpack. Everything he needed was on his laptop inside that ratty thing he refused to replace ("Bren, it was a gift from you and look, it's over a decade old and still holding on!"), but digging all that out now made Clark wonder if he'd look unapproachable.

His coffee was only half gone when Jasper walked into the cafe. Clark's breath caught. Jasper always looked good. Every time he was in the library, Jasper looked like he'd just come from orchestra practice or lessons with one of his students; professional but always with a certain flair that made Clark think of Parisian fashion runways. One day a delicate scarf with tassels that looked like spun gold, then the next time Jasper was in a tight turtleneck that hid very little of his body and was accentuated by bold jewelry. But now he wore dark blue jeans, brown boots, and a deep purple sweater that looked both soft and on the edge of too tight. His long blond hair was down and he wore glasses with thin gold frames. He was pretty sure the guy seated to the left of the door sighed when Jasper walked in.

Jasper stepped out of the way of the entrance, paused to look around, and when he caught sight of Clark, a lazy smirk slid over his face. He waved and walked over, moving faster now that he'd seen Clark. Clark's heart kicked up the moment their eyes met, and Clark could feel it banging about beneath his ribs.

"I do love people who are mindful of the time," Jasper said as he slid into the booth. "Have you been waiting long?"

Clark motioned to his half-empty cup. "Only long enough to get this in me."

"A man after my own heart. Caffeine first, then business."

Something about Jasper was softer, easier tonight. He was always politely charming when he came into the library, but tonight his tone was almost a drawl. It lit up something in Clark's brain, made him clench the hand resting on his thigh. "I was going to get a refill. What do you want?"

"A flat white. And here." Jasper handed him a few bills.

Clark shook his head. "My treat. You can get me next time."

The smirk was back and it lingered while Jasper settled into the booth, one arm over the top of it. Looking utterly at ease. "Then I appreciate it. And next time will be more than coffee, I promise."

"Right. Yeah. That's...thanks." Clark got up, feeling a little unsteady in the ebb of Jasper's attention. "Be right back."

"I'll be here."

Clark took a few deep breaths as he went to the counter. Jasper was making him feel all kinds of things and he'd only been in the cafe two minutes. Either Jasper was flirting - *was that flirting?* - or Clark was fooling himself. For a moment, he wished he could ask Bren what she thought. And he could already hear her replying to *be himself* because no one deserved him any other way.

Clark sighed, smiled at the woman behind the counter, and ordered, wondering if the butterflies in his stomach were all of the excited variety. He fought the urge to look over his shoulder, but as the woman came back with their cups, she chuckled and said, "First date?"

"Uh...I'm not sure." Clark could feel his cheeks heating up.

She shrugged, making her long gold hoops jangle. "I think your friend thinks it is. That guy hasn't taken his eyes off you since you got up."

Now his face was burning. "Oh. Okay."

She smiled and strode off, leaving him to toddle back to the table with two very full cups.

"Ah, lovely," Jasper said, taking the cups from him with long, graceful fingers. *Don't look at his hands. You'll fixate and spill the drinks.* When the cups were safely on the table, Jasper turned to him, curiosity lighting his green eyes. "So, I have to say I'm excited about planning this Haven ghost hunt. I've always gone on these things alone, and it'll be nice to explore with a friend." In a rare moment of hesitation,

Jasper frowned. "Is it okay if I call you that? A friend, I mean. I realize we don't know each other very well."

Clark's throat was full of sawdust and disbelief. "I would like that, actually," he managed to reply before taking a big gulp of his coffee. The scalding liquid hit his tongue and immediately went down wrong, leaving him sputtering and coughing into his fist. He heard Jasper mutter something and then a warm hand was rubbing his back, coaxing him through his fit. His eyes burned with tears, his throat was on fire, but all Clark could feel was that hand on his back.

"Are you all right?" Jasper hovered close, concerned.

"Fine, just..." Clark coughed again before sinking back against the booth. "Pro tip, don't drink it scalding hot like that."

"Let me get you some water." Before Clark could protest, Jasper was up and at the counter. The same woman who had taken his order quickly handed over a small plastic cup of water, and then Jasper was at his side once more, concern etched on his fine features. This close, Clark could smell him - coffee and spice and...sugar, which was interesting but sort of perfect. "Can you drink this?"

Clark nodded and took a few small sips to calm his throat. "Thanks. Okay, I'm off to a great start, I guess."

Jasper smiled. "You're doing fine." He didn't touch Clark again, which was unfortunate. "Ready to continue?"

"Yes, of course." From their bags they pulled laptops and notebooks and Jasper spread a small map out between them. "Oh, perfect!" Clark said, pleasantly surprised at the depth of Jasper's planning. "I love these maps PhantasmaScreams does for their hunts."

"You'd mentioned you'd been on other hunts with this group." Jasper traced his finger over the PhantasmaScreams logo in the bottom left corner. "How did you get started with them?"

"Actually a long time ago, when they were doing videos on camcorders and putting them up on some of those early internet platforms."

"Twine? Or Capture?"

Clark beamed. "Capture. Gods, what a relic of its age now. But yeah, they used to do videos around their town, just college kids with a penchant for ghost stories. They did it for the thrills, initially, and I wasn't into that. But they arranged a group outing at this abandoned cemetery about two years into their video making, after they blew up on some of the big chat boards at the time. I went, since it was close to here, and..." Clark blew out a sigh. "I definitely witnessed *something* that night. Light and cold and this unshakeable sensation I was being watched." He shook his head, took another sip of his coffee. The sudden recall of memory, the power of that moment, rushed back at him. He gave Jasper a sheepish smile. "Sorry. I haven't talked about this in a while."

Jasper studied him over the rim of his own cup. That look, that softness on Jasper's face, felt like someone caressing his cheek. Clark wanted to lean into it, relish it. And when Jasper spoke, his voice had gone thick and syrupy and it dropped into Clark's ears like a perfectly tuned orchestra. "You have nothing to apologize for. I like your passion, your enthusiasm. You show it at your job and you share it with everyone who comes up to you for help." Jasper arched an eyebrow, grinning. "You certainly have given me some very good book recommendations. Even unseated a few of my favorite books for new ones."

"You can't dangle that in front of me and not spill," Clark said, leaning forward.

Jasper laughed. "Ah, for starters, *To Turn A Forge*. I never knew I needed a fantasy book about a lesbian blacksmith and their metal-bending magic before." If Jasper realized he was leaning in, he didn't make any more to pull back. He was so close now, Clark could feel air move as Jasper said, "Incredible book. Top five of all time for me."

"I knew you would love that one. It's so unique but *so* well written. And you said you love a good turn of phrase. That author has a penchant for it."

"I really do. And I love the way you say that word."

Clark frowned. "What word?"

"*Penchant.*" Jasper rolled the word around, let it drape off his tongue in the way only a native French speaker could. Clark considered swooning, especially because Jasper was now leaning on the table and his sweater bunched in all the right places. Like over his biceps. "Honestly, I enjoy listening to you talk, especially when you're into something. I would say I find your Midwestern accent charming but I don't want to offend."

Clark could barely get the word out. "Offend?"

"When people find out I lived in France until I was seven, they then tell me how beautiful my voice is, how I pronounce words. It used to bother me. It felt like they were reducing my life to an early childhood in a country I have not visited since." He shrugged, trying to look casual but Clark could see a bit of tension around his mouth, fine lines straining against the smooth surface of his skin. "It's a silly thing, but I'm rather aware of how others might feel if I said something similar to them." The intensity of the moment hung in the silence between them, then Jasper said, "And I've gotten us off track."

"I really don't mind." If Clark was fumbling his words, it was only because he wanted to stay in this spot and just *talk* to Jasper. Let them be the last ones out the door, let their conversation take them down sidewalks to that late-night noodle shop on the corner of Fifth and Lane.

Let it take them back to his house and into his bed and...

"You are very thoughtful. And kind," Jasper said softly.

"You're going to make me blush," Clark replied, trying not to do that very thing.

"Hmmm, maybe not tonight. But I'd love another try at it."

Jasper was a goddamn *tease* and Clark was so into it. As a distraction, Clark tapped the map and said, "We are going on a ghost hunt together."

"We are." Jasper gave a thoughtful tap to his chin. "Perhaps I should try it out there. See if the cold or my words bring a first bit of pink to your cheeks."

Swooning was *definitely* still on the table.

"Right so uh..." Clark looked away, momentarily overcome. God, Jasper was so good looking and funny and Clark was in big trouble. "Camping and ghost hunt planning?"

Jasper gave him a soft, sweet smile. "Back on track. Perfect librarianship, the stewarding of tasks and time. I put myself in your capable hands, Clark."

I'm going to bed with the biggest grin tonight. Clark squirmed in his seat. *And possibly the biggest hard-on.*

One week later; one week until the ghost hunt and Flannery's speed dating night

"So, you're still going to the speed dating thing?" Clark stared at his sister, agog.

"Yeah, why not?"

"Bren, you have a date."

"No, I have a friend who wants to come with me."

Clark gave Bren a long-suffering look before spearing a cherry tomato onto his fork. "You have a *new* friend who just so happens to want to tag along. At a speed dating event. At a bar. A bar, might I add, that's famous for bathroom stall hookups."

Bren snorted into her water glass. "I am not, and will never, hook up with anyone in any room that involves a toilet. And besides, where do you get off, Mr. 'I'm just going on a camping trip with Hot Glasses guy from my work'?"

For emphasis - and because he knew it would make her glare - Clark retorted with, "I never said it *wasn't* a date. We were never specific."

"Ugh. The *absence of a thing* argument again?" Bren looked like she might bang her head onto the table. "Please, no. Mercy. I give."

Clark chuckled and went back to his plate. Bren had charcoal grilled chicken kebabs and they were perfect, so he was trying to savor them, but it was difficult. He'd already inhaled one; it had been much needed after someone pulling a fire alarm at the library led to a building evacuation and a two-hour inspection by the fire department. While they all waited in the cold.

"Well, then I guess we're both stuck, huh?" he asked while Bren refilled their waters. He raised his. "To being stuck. Here is better than what we'd been stuck in before."

"True." Bren clinked her glass against his, a slight smile stealing over her face. "I like Elodie a lot. She's been a good collaboration partner. Iris is over the moon to not have to deal with research for the podcast. And we're recording the next episode soon."

Clark perked up. The plans Bren and Iris had for their podcast were quietly ambitious. Not surprising, given his sister's passion for plants but lack of time to do any in-depth research. She had tons of books on plant folklore and mythology, many of them belonging to their mother, but never had the chance to really dive in. He'd offered to help a few times, but Bren had just said she'd "get to it someday" and told him not to worry. Clark was really proud of Bren's sudden openness. Maybe a new friend was what she'd needed. "When are you recording?"

"Next Monday at two. Elodie's got class until noon and Iris has to run Sam over to his dad's at five, so it'll be a short one. A good test for all of us, I think."

"So...just friends-only vibes?"

That seemed to bring his sister up short. Her pause was long and weighted. "I'm not sure," Bren finally replied. "We just haven't had enough time together. You know I'm slow to warm up to people."

"You say that, but you and Iris clicked immediately." Clark held up his hands to ward her off. "But I also know you said that was really unique for you."

"It was." Bren smiled. "But you know Iris is like a sister to me."

"Yeah."

After a few quiet minutes, Bren gathered up her dishes and held her hand out for Clark's. He passed them over and started to pick up the rest of the table, when Bren said, "So you'll be gone next Friday afternoon through Sunday morning?"

"Yeah. At least that, because sometimes things happen at these hunts and there's documentation to do. Why?"

Bren gave a one-shouldered shrug. "It'll be weird to have the house so quiet."

Clark couldn't resist. "Are you saying I'm loud?"

Now came the tiniest smile, so small it was almost a secret between them. "I don't know what you're talking about."

"Oh no, of course not."

Bren flipped him the middle finger but started laughing, so Clark did, too. It was nice to see his sister smiling like that, and he couldn't help but think it was because of this new woman in her life. Maybe something good would come out of the weekend for both of them.

Chapter Seven

Speed dating night at Flannery's

"What the hell do you wear to these things?" Bren gestured at her dirt-streaked work pants, then to her closet. "I don't go to *events*."

Iris groaned dramatically and flung herself back on Bren's bed. "Girl. Bren, I love you, but you didn't think about this before? What did you wear last time?"

"Black pants, boots, a nice button-down shirt, and Mom's sapphire necklace."

Iris groaned again. "Okay, the necklace and black pants are good. Everything else is not so great. You don't have *anything* in there? I'm sure my shirts would fit you but not any of my pants. Your legs are too long."

Bren gestured at her closet and the sparse number of hangers inside. "It's kind of a desert in there but you're welcome to dig."

At that, Iris launched herself up and into the closet, going right for the back where some plastic totes were kept. "What's in here?"

Bren paused, racking her memory. "Uh, maybe some old clothes? Shoes? I'm not sure."

"I'm gonna find out."

Bren got out of the way as Iris tore into her closet. It was easier to fuss over the things she knew were definite – black pants, Mom's necklace, the state of her long, frizzy, dark hair. Iris had given her a small tub of pomade, so Bren went to the bathroom and began to rub a tiny amount of the sweet-smelling stuff into the worst places. Because her hair was always pulled up for work, Bren didn't mess with it much. There was no need for pomade when her hair would come into contact with water, dirt, sweat, and all manner of plant matter. And since it had been that way for years, Bren had gotten into a simple daily routine and liked it. She wasn't out of her depths for tonight, necessarily; she knew what mascara and lip gloss were, for fuck's sake. She just never really *bothered*.

"Ouch."

"You okay?" Bren peered into the closet.

"Fine. Just smacked my head...ah, what's this?" There was a moment of silence and then Iris crawled out of the closet with something the color of lilacs in her hand. "Bren! This!" And she shoved the gauzy thing at Bren like it was buried treasure. "You have to show off those arms you have. Someone will *definitely* swoon."

Bren gave the blouse a skeptical look. "Where the hell did you find this? I don't think I've ever worn it."

"Buried! Buried in that blue tote in the back of your closet. It was folded up inside a nice jacket. Which..." Iris dove back into the closet only to reappear with said jacket in hand. "This is also something I'd recommend. I know you run hot, so if you park close to the bar, you can forgo all that awkwardness around a coat."

Bren shook out the shirt and jacket. "I think I bought this jacket for a wedding."

"Yeah?"

She snorted. "It never happened. It was an old college friend's wedding and they broke up two weeks before they went to the altar. I must have shoved this out of the way and just forgot."

Iris was instantly on her feet and standing before her, hands on Bren's shoulders. "Trust me on this one." She gave Bren's hair a once-over with a grin. "That pomade is killer. Your hair looks like you just got laid in that sexy, lazy kind of way."

Despite herself, Bren laughed. "You are ridiculous."

Iris hugged her and Bren accepted that warmth and love with open arms. "Yep, but when it comes to you, I'm not messing around." Iris stepped back, still smiling. "I'll let you get changed, but I'm not leaving until you look perfect."

Iris closed the bedroom door behind her and Bren stared at the clothes on her bed with a sigh. The sleeveless lilac blouse looked so flimsy. She was used to clothes and shoes that could take a beating, and that blouse appeared to be made of tissue paper and hope.

Well, here goes, she thought as she dumped her work clothes into the hamper in the bathroom and took a five-minute shower before pulling everything on. Shockingly, every piece still fit, though the jacket was a tiny bit tight around the shoulders. She'd lifted *a lot* of bags of mulch and dirt since college. But it had deep pockets and hung past her hips, so Bren didn't feel like she'd be worried about her ass not being covered. She'd probably wind up focused on how thin the sleeveless shirt felt, like she wasn't wearing anything, but the jacket would help with that.

When Bren examined herself in the bathroom mirror, what she saw was serviceable. Hair still slightly frizzy. It was more of an office look than casual or flirty, but the mere thought of wearing a dress made her want to put on sweats and not leave the house. Bren fished her mom's necklace out of the shirt and let the lights hit it until it glowed. It was a pretty thing; a silver filigree pendant with a perfectly cut, dark blue sapphire in the center.

Iris was right. The blue in the gem blended nicely with the light purple blouse. Subtle but eye-catching if you got close enough. And Bren had a pretty good idea on who Iris thought was going to be *close* like that tonight.

Bren gave herself a moment of truth while staring at her reflection. She liked Elodie. She'd been surprised Elodie wanted to come along for the event, but the woman managed to confound Bren's expectations at every turn.

"I think we're all set," Elodie said as she shut her portfolio and smiled at Iris and Bren. "All that's left is to figure out when to record. I hate to sound eager, but I'd love to do it this week. Even Friday or Saturday."

Bren started to nod but Iris nudged her. "Can't on Friday, either of us," Iris replied quickly. "I've got my kiddo for the weekend and Bren's got a thing."

Elodie smiled at Bren. "A thing?"

Bren wanted to groan but Elodie seemed genuinely curious. "A speed dating thing at Flannery's downtown. I'm trying to be more social," Bren said, trying to not sound too self-effacing.

"Oh! I've not been to that! Do they do it often?"

Iris shook her head. "They just started back up. I'm so glad Bren's going, it'll get her out of the house."

"Hey, unfair," Bren shot back with a small smile. "I leave the house. I work!"

"And where else do you go?"

"The grocery store, the farm store-"

Iris leaned over to Elodie and stage whispered, "Yeah, and that's it."

"Rude." Bren tugged on Iris's braid. "Anyways, I'm trying things out. The dating apps were a bust."

"I hate those things," Elodie said. "So fake."

Bren caught Iris's stare out of the corner of her eye. She could feel in her gut what was coming and, like standing in front of a train, figured she might as well let it happen. It couldn't hurt to have a friend with her for speed dating, right? "I uh...you can come along, if you want to," Bren said to Elodie, who immediately beamed at her. "Might make it less awkward."

"And keep you from standing in the corner for two hours," Iris said, poking Bren in the thigh.

"Are you sure?" Elodie asked as she fiddled with her pen. "I don't want to intrude."

"No intrusion. I would like the company." Bren dug her phone out of her pocket. "I'll text you the details."

"Well, now I'm very excited to have plans on Friday night. I was considering what shitty movie I'd watch and now I don't have to decide." Something in Elodie's tone made Bren's heart beat a little harder. "And if the event sucks, we can just hang out together. Have some drinks."

Bren swallowed hard. "Yeah. I'd like that."

They couldn't be more different. But there was a sensitive soul in Elodie and Bren admired her positivity, her enthusiasm for...for *life*. It tugged on Bren in a way that felt foreign but nice at the same time.

She *could* do this. The worst that could happen would be the speed dates would be a bust, and she and Elodie could belly up to the bar and just talk. *When was the last time I did that? I can't even remember.*

"Hey, Iris!"

Her friend immediately was there, poking her head around the corner and getting her first look at Bren. "Okay. Whoa. You look killer."

"Be serious."

"I absolutely fucking *am*." Iris held up her hands. "I know you don't like to be gushed over. But straight up, you look great. That lilac suits you really well, Bren." Bren let Iris fuss over her, straightening her clothes, adding more pomade to her hair, even running a tiny brush over her thick eyebrows. "I would date you," Iris said when she was done. "Dead serious."

"Stop. I'm going to blush," Bren deadpanned, making Iris laugh.

"Wouldn't want that." Iris glanced at the clock on the bedroom wall. "Time to go, girlie. Your car will be here soon."

Bren's phone buzzed on the chipped countertop and she snatched it up when she saw Elodie's name.

From: Elodie *Ready? I'm so excited!*

From: Bren *Yeah, my car's almost here, and then we'll come to you.*

From: Elodie *The car was such a good idea. I get tipsy after two martinis.*

From: Bren *Fancy. I have to get about 6 beers in me before I feel it. And I'm not big on beer.*

From: Elodie *Remind me to not challenge you with drinking in any way.*

From: Bren *I wouldn't recommend it. I held some records in college. Which, looking back, was not a good or healthy thing.*

From: Elodie *Maybe not, but I'd love to hear about it if you're willing to share. We can swap stories at the bar if the speed dating busts.*

Chuckling, Bren tucked her phone away, accepted Iris's hug, and went outside her house to wait for her ride to show. At the very least, this night wouldn't be a complete waste of time if she got to know Elodie a bit more.

If Elodie didn't walk away from tonight with at least one date, Bren would eat her shoes. The woman's love of color was muted, but that didn't mean she blended in. The opposite, actually.

And Bren was staring. Hard.

She hadn't seen Elodie's outfit in the car and Elodie hadn't seen hers, as both of them had been bundled up against the chill spring rain. But after they got their speed dating question cards from the greeter, Elodie took Bren's coat to the tiny coat check room ("Fancy for a pub!" Elodie had exclaimed, delighted).

And then she came back and Bren's entire world screeched to a halt.

Elodie *glittered*. Her tiny frame was wrapped in a satin jumpsuit the color of champagne and she strode across the pub floor in high heels, swaying with the kind of confidence Bren had never mastered. There was nothing scandalous or even daring about the jumpsuit and Elodie's heels were tall but not towering. But she *shone* and it left Bren gaping. And she wasn't the only one watching Elodie glide back to their table with an energy that brought them all like moths to her flame.

"Oh, Bren!" Elodie grinned at Bren, her pearl drop earrings swinging slightly with her movements. "I love that lilac blouse on you! It's a good color against your dark hair."

Bren shifted from foot to foot. She wasn't used to compliments and Elodie's seemed especially genuine. *Enjoy it*, she could hear her brother saying. *Elodie's nice, she's fun to talk to. Let tonight take you wherever it leads.* "Thanks," Bren replied, running a hand over her hair. "Iris actually found it in my closet, so the credit should go to her."

"Well, it really makes your eyes pop. And it goes so well with that beautiful pendant." Elodie leaned forward slightly, looking up at Bren. Bren's neck, specifically, where the necklace hung below the hollow of her throat. "God, that filigree work on the pendant is wildly intricate. It reminds me of ivy."

Bren froze. Her mother had said something similar when she and Clark had given the necklace to her, bought with earnings from their first jobs at sixteen. Clark had worked as a bagger at the grocery store, wanting to be around people and chatter. And Bren had opted to work the zip lines at a kid's adventure park on the other side of town, preferring to deal with the kids and let her manager handle any parent complaints. Plus, that meant she got to be outdoors, and if it rained, she could go to the gear shed and help the college kids clean equipment.

They'd put a little away from each paycheck so that they could buy their parents something special on their birthdays. That necklace had been their first gift like that to their mother. It would be only one of three they would get to purchase before she passed away. Her hand went to it, as if she could ward off the sudden flood of emotions.

Immediately, Elodie sensed something was wrong. She reached across the table but didn't touch Bren. "Bren. Do you want to tell me what's wrong, or do you need to step outside?"

"No." Bren shook her head. Her mother had been gone for eighteen years. And still there were days that felt like the wound had opened once more. "I just..." She swallowed hard, then reached for the water pitcher and glasses on the table. "You said something really close to what my mom used to say about the necklace," Bren said after taking several sips. "Clark and I bought it for her when we were sixteen. She wore it until she passed and then it came back to me." Bren reached to the necklace again, the calluses on her fingertips catching against the fine silver.

Elodie was quietly watching her, that two-toned gaze intent but not intrusive. "It looks good on you, just like I'm sure it did on her." Elodie shifted in her seat and Bren watched the light play over her jumpsuit. "I appreciate you sharing that with me."

Bren didn't quite know what to say, and when a waiter bustled by to take their drink orders, she managed to give Elodie a small, genuine smile.

"Well, shall we?" Elodie asked after they ordered, gesturing to their questionnaires. "And we should probably scope out who's here."

"It's like a weird form of people watching," Bren said, her eyes going to her paper. "We're all staring at each other, trying to see who we click with from a look. And since that never happens anywhere but in the movies, it feels so..." She huffed through her nose, mostly at her ever-persistent cynicism. "Sorry. I really am going to try tonight." And she handed Elodie a golf pencil before taking one for herself.

They worked through the first few questions in silence, until Bren saw question number five.

- **What do you hope to find tonight? Pick all that apply.**

  ○ **Meeting new people**

  ○ **Interesting conversation**

  ○ **Friendship**

  ○ **A date**

  ○ **Nothing specific/keeping it casual**

  ○ **Other (please specify)**

Good question, Bren thought. *Can I write, "I don't know, all of the above but also I kind of miss physical intimacy and wouldn't mind taking someone home?"*

"Okay, these are...pretty standard but oof, number eight. Favorite book? Like I'm supposed to pick that!" Elodie glanced at Bren's paper and must have noticed her hesitation. "Stuck?"

"Five's got me hung up. Think I can skip it?"

"Please don't skip questions!" Sasha, the event's regular host, a statuesque person with bright red hair and a killer green dress, walked by. "We need these to help match you up! This quiz was made by a dating app designer so I can guarantee that we need these answers." Sasha had deep gold highlighter on their cheeks and it sparkled like Elodie's jumpsuit.

I must have been a magpie in another life, Bren thought as she ripped her gaze away. "Sorry. Yeah, I'll...do my best."

"Great!" Sasha smiled, all bright white teeth and curving lips. "That's all I ask." They paused, eyes narrowed. "Wait, I know you."

Immediately, Bren's stomach dropped to the floor, and then fell below, into the earth. *No no no, c'mon...*

"Yeah!" Sasha's grin widened and now instead of an attractive expression, Bren swore it took on an edge of glee. She held her hands out imploringly and thankfully, Sasha seemed to understand. "You're the mushroom lady! I'm tickled you're here, really." They'd kept their voice down now but Bren was still drawing a few looks. God, she wanted to hide.

Not this again. Please not all the attention and staring and eyes following me. I saved a coworker and a friend, that was it. I helped. It wasn't anything special. EMTs and firefighters and nurses save people all the time.

I did nothing special.

Please stop staring.

I can feel all of them looking, digging out their phones and racing to go find the video online.

Please, PLEASE stop staring.

"Bren?" A warm hand curled around hers, the grip firm and grounding. "Hey. Why don't we go outside for some air? We can finish those questionnaires later."

Bren shook her head. Her eyes felt cloudy, her head foggy. And while her heart slammed hard in her chest, she tried to breathe like her therapist had taught her. In and out, slowly and evenly. But that panic was welling, surging in her chest.

She had to go.

She had to go.

"Sorry. For the car and drinks," she mumbled as she blindly shoved a few bills at Elodie and ran for the door. The slap of wind didn't do anything to shake Bren from her fog. Were her hands shaking from anxiety and stress, or from the cold? Trembling, Bren pulled her phone from her crossbody bag and took off down the sidewalk, the rideshare app pulled up and waiting for her request.

"Bren! Bren!"

Bren didn't want to turn, but the voice in the back of her mind that sounded like her mother told her it would be rude otherwise. But she didn't say anything, simply looked over her shoulder and saw Elodie running at her, both of their coats in hand.

She should keep walking. Elodie didn't need to be witness to her failings and fumblings, her sheer fucking *inability* to deal when someone recognized her from that *goddamn commercial*.

Bren stopped. Tried to breathe. Looked back and saw Elodie's glittering outline and the deep concern written all over her face.

"Hey." Elodie held out Bren's coat. With a nod, Bren took it. "Do you want me to get you a ride home?"

Home was *exactly* where Bren needed to be. There, she was safe. There, she was just *Bren*. Even with Clark gone for the weekend, Bren could curl up on the couch in the main house and wrap blankets around herself, poke her fingers into the holes in fabric she knew well.

But alone wasn't maybe a good idea. What if she started thinking and worrying? Then she'd go online and start obsessively searching for any "mushroom lady sightings".

"Bren? It's okay if you can't talk, or don't want to. Can you look at me, so I know you can hear me?"

Elodie's voice was soothing on Bren's jangling nerves. She sucked in a deep breath and nodded. "I can hear you." Her own voice sounded foreign to her ears; scratching and scraping like dragging her throat through gravel.

"Okay, good." Elodie held out her phone so Bren could see the screen. "That's your address, right?"

"Yes." *Home* was the balm to the frantic beat of her heart, the jump of her pulse under her skin. *Home* was safe and there Bren could let everything go.

"Okay. I'm calling for a car so we can get you home." Elodie edged closer. "Is that all right?"

Bren nodded. "I can talk," she said. "Just not...not well right now." She didn't dare look Elodie's way again. Pity she could handle; sympathy was false pity, dressed up to appear more polite. "Thanks for the car."

"Sure." Elodie paused, twisting her hands together. Bren noticed Elodie had slipped into her coat, while Bren's was dangling over her own arm. She didn't want it, but there was a fine mist in the air and it made her bones ache. "Do you want help with your coat?"

"I'm not a toddler," Bren grumbled.

"I know. I'm just asking." Palm up to the sky, Elodie held her hand out to the mist like an offering. Bren watched as water droplets collected on Elodie's skin – her fingertips, the ridge of her thumb, her wrist. The water glistened in the streetlights overhead. "Car should be here soon."

"Okay."

Silence hung between them.

Bren didn't know what to say. She no longer felt panicked but something in her very being jumped at every sound, every shadow. She was on "high alert", as Dr. Marshall would say. Flight or fight had nothing on Bren's ability to be aware of everything and nothing at the same time.

Finding monsters in every corner. That's what some of us see when we go through trauma. Our system builds in alarms, and we suffer through the symptoms of it. Increased heart rate and breathing, sweating, chills, nausea, brain fog. Some people completely shut down. But you, Bren...you go back to comfort. You flee, yes, but where you flee is home. And you've admitted you don't like being alone.

A red electric vehicle pulled up next to them. "Here we go," Elodie said as she held open the door for Bren. "Can I text you later, just to make sure you're okay? I'm worried, Bren. And I'm sorry for that but - "

"You can come with, if you want." Bren still couldn't quite look Elodie's way, so she fixated on the spotless, black leather interior of the car. "I owe you."

Elodie scoffed at that. "You don't."

"No I...I definitely do."

"All right. I'll come." She waved Bren forward. "After you ."

The finality of the car door slamming shut was only surmounted by how close Elodie had to press to fit into the small car. Knees, outer thighs, hips, elbows...all against each together in a mockery of the hug Bren was gathering the courage to ask for.

Chapter Eight

From: Jasper I stopped to put gas in the car. Do you
need anything? Last minute snacks, extra lighter, etc?

The text came in just as Clark put down his window to greet the
smiling young woman wearing a lime green beanie. "Hey there! I just
need to scan your ticket."

"Sure." Clark turned his phone toward her. When her handheld
scanner beeped, green light on the device blinking bright in the dull
gray afternoon, he nodded. "I'm not too early, am I?"

She grinned. "Nope! We're at about half capacity already, actually.
Though I guess that makes sense, with the rain coming in." The
woman wrinkled her nose as she looked to the sky. "Not a downpour
but it's gonna make things pretty damp. Hope you brought everything
you need. Once the rain starts, the fields turn to mud and the drive out
can get a bit bumpy."

"I'm good but thanks."

"Okay, cool! You're in spot twelve. Head up to the split in the road,
go left, and then left again. It's pretty isolated, so it'll just be you and
spots thirteen through fifteen. That still okay?"

"Absolutely." Clark smiled back at her, unable to stop the little ribbon of excitement wandering through him. "I know the man in spot thirteen."

"Heck yeah. Ghost huntin' friends. Well, you're all set. Have fun!"

"Thanks." Once his window was back up, Clark took a moment to get his bearings. The ghost hunting site was on a massive, wooded lot that had been donated to a local history group. Two very old cemeteries abutted the acreage, one on the north side and the other on the far eastern side. The camping grounds for hunts were kept away from those spots, by request of the history group. You could visit them during the hunt, but couldn't camp nearby. And while some attendees grumbled at this, it wasn't as though the woods were lacking for stories of the supernatural. The energy was palpable, and Clark was hoping tonight it would manifest.

When he got to the designated campsite, he was finally able to answer Jasper's text with an affirmative, "I'm good, but thanks". A thumbs-up emoji followed.

Chuckling, Clark put his phone away before beginning his site set-up. It was a routine he knew well by now and his gear was well-used but well-maintained, so setting up was easily done by himself. The PhantasmaScreams team always provided fire starters and wood, bear-proof trash bins, and had supplies on hand to help out should something go awry. It wasn't roughing it, but it wasn't glamping, which was perfect in Clark's opinion. He wanted to focus on the energy, the stories, the *place*, instead of worrying about firewood.

As Clark went through his routine, he wondered when, or if, he should divulge certain information to Jasper. Yes, he was out here to see or experience something supernatural. That was always the goal. He cared not a bit about documenting it; chasing internet clout was never anywhere close to Clark's priority list. And after years and years of introspection and probably too many books on the subject, Clark had decided he was seeking *closure*.

Did one ever fully escape the death of a loved one?

Dad's stroke when he and Bren were ten. Mom's car accident when they were almost twenty. All that time apart meant nothing in the wake of crushing sadness. For both he and Bren, those losses might as well have been back-to-back.

Clark had always believed in the supernatural. He'd once asked his parents if a certain cartoon ghost was real and if so, could they invite him over for a sleepover. That was childish whimsy. This.... this was a passion. A cause. A belief stronger than any he might have for a deity.

Clark knew his parents were gone. But his heart told him maybe, just maybe, he could hear them once more if he found the right frequency.

Tires on gravel caught his attention and Clark looked over his shoulder to see a small SUV pull up in spot thirteen. "Hey there," he said once Jasper had hopped out of his vehicle. "I like the hat."

Jasper tapped the black waterproof bucket hat with a gloved finger. "I wasn't sure if the strap under my chin made it better or worse in appearance, but at least it won't slide off my head."

"Hmmm, hold on." Clark stepped up to Jasper, keeping a respectful distance but close enough that he could see the hat better. "I like it. Makes you look like you're going out in the wilderness with purpose."

"Well, if it gets your vote, then I'll keep it." Jasper motioned to Clark's tent. "Ah, no one told me it was fancy tent season."

"My cube is not fancy. It's a cube."

Jasper gave the gray and orange tent the once-over. Clark felt as though he was also being scrutinized, in a strange kind of way. "It's a waterproof cube tent with its own umbrella. It's impressive. Clearly you know what you're doing."

Clark tried not to beam at the praise. "Well, then can I give you a hand? I figured I'd wait until the mist stopped before starting a fire."

"I'd love that."

Together they set up Jasper's tent, then the rest of the campsite. Clark found talking to Jasper was easy. It felt natural. Usually, small talk made him clam up. Sure, he talked to people as part of his job, but in more casual social situations, Clark had a tendency to keep to himself or to converse with one or two other people. Neither he nor Bren were exactly social butterflies, even if she insisted he was a natural conversationalist. Clark liked to think it was rigorous practice that gave him any skill in that regard. After all, if you could talk a patron down off the top of the shelves in the local history section, you could probably make a few polite comments about the punch at a party.

"Hey, Jasper? Where do you want this duffel bag? Should I leave it in the car?"

"Just hand it to me, thanks."

Jasper appeared at Clark's side, hand outstretched. "Where did the hat go?" Clark asked as he passed over the bag, trying not to stare at Jasper's hair. It hung loose in waves around his face, highlighting an angular jaw and making Jasper's green eyes look black in the bleak afternoon light.

"It turns out the strap was making my neck itch and I apparently have a different definition of *waterproof* than the scammy company that made that abomination of a hat." But Jasper didn't look bothered one bit. "So, I'll bravely forgo the hat. Especially now that we're set up. Which means..." He shook the bag. "I brought a small kettle and some tea, if you'd like to share with me while we wait for twilight."

"Looks like hot drinks are our thing."

Clark was teasing but Jasper gave a serious nod. "I hope it's not the only thing."

Clark's throat was so dry now. "Books, of course."

Jasper took a step forward, bag clanking at his side. "Of course. And ghost hunts."

The cold air felt too warm. He was too warm, actually, so Clark pulled off his knit beanie. "A good list."

"So far." Jasper winked. *Winked.* "And your tea choice is about to tell me quite a lot, so…"

Clark laughed, knowing he was red in the cheeks and not caring. "If you tell me you read tea leaves, I'll have to marry you."

"Afraid I don't," Jasper replied with another full-bodied laugh. "I think you're the more crafty, creative type in some regard. For example…" Jasper pointed to Clark's hat. "Did you make that?"

Give me an observant man who knows hand-knit over machine-made any day, and can switch topics with such ease you'd think he was oiled. "I did." Without invitation, Clark held it out. While Jasper gingerly turned the hat over in his hands, Clark walked over to stoke the fire. "Knitting was something for my hands to do when I first started working in libraries. It was this tiny place, one stoplight kind of town."

"That is very small."

Clark gave a shrug but laughed. "It's the Midwest, there are still a lot of places like that." He gestured around them. "Especially further north." When Jasper nodded, Clark kept going. "So, on the days where we'd go hours without anyone coming in, our options were to stare at the wall or read. And sometimes I simply wasn't in the mood to focus on a book."

Jasper's snort-laugh was the cutest thing Clark had ever heard. "Let me guess, every time you got to a really good part, someone would come in?"

"Give the man a prize," Clark deadpanned.

When Clark looked up, he realized Jasper had come closer again, this time to sit beside him on the rough-hewn log bench. "Do I get to pick my winnings?" Jasper asked while leaning in. With their height difference terribly obvious even seated, Clark had a hard time not biting his lip. It was insanely sexy, the way Jasper loomed over him.

All Clark could do was swallow hard and say, "Sure. Within reason."

"Of course." *Oh, fuck him*, Clark thought viciously. He wasn't the type to make the first move and he was pretty damn sure Jasper *was exactly the type*. "I'll think about it. Don't let me interrupt your story anymore. I have a bad habit of steering conversations off track. Apologies for that."

Clark found himself transfixed with the way the little notch at the right upper corner of Jasper's lip danced with his smile. His heart was beating *hard*. Surely Jasper heard it. Clark felt like the entire *campground* could hear it and they'd all come running to see what was going on. "No need to apologize," Clark croaked out, trying to unscramble the neurons in his brain, so he could focus on anything but how quickly he'd gotten flustered over a bit of flirting.

Dark settled around them like Clark's favorite wool camping blanket – heavy but comforting. It was time to put their plan for the first night into action. No cameras, no fancy gadgets, just their safety gear, backpacks with essentials like snacks and thermoses full of tea, and little Xs on a paper map (but they had their phones and GPS, too). Old school. Exactly Clark's speed.

Clark was zipping up his backpack when Jasper came out of his tent with a frown. "Something wrong?"

"I keep feeling a draft in my tent but I can't understand from where." Jasper shone his flashlight over the tent entrance. "Do you see anything?"

"Let's check." They spent the next few minutes scouring the tent's fabric for any holes but found nothing. "Sorry," Clark said with a gentle, reassuring pat to Jasper's shoulder.

"Then I guess I best hope it doesn't rain."

Clark's bold response was so automatic, it shocked even him. "I've plenty of room, if it comes to that."

"You are very kind. But I wouldn't ask that."

"And you didn't." Clark gave the tent another once-over. "But between the hat and the tent, I think your gauge for good gear needs tuning."

Jasper flicked the flashlight off with a chuckle. In the thick twilight, the purples and blues and blacks of the sky turned his blond hair and green eyes into shadows. There was an enticing look on the man's face, as if he wanted to beckon Clark closer. As if he simply *wanted* Clark near him. They were standing close already, and Clark could feel that *tease* building again. "You are very kind," Jasper repeated. His voice sounded darker now, deeper.

"We'll see if you still think that by the night's end." Clark flashed him a smile. "I have a tendency to traipse through about anything to try to get a better look at what's out there."

"Sounds fun. I'm in."

Clark jostled his pack and fought the urge to squirm. This man was delicately tearing his insides to shreds and gods help him, Clark liked it. "Off we go, then."

The hiking path closest to their campsite was the reason Clark had chosen this spot - it went up and around the woods for miles and miles, and ended at a small clearing bordering a pond. "The story is that the lake was popular with people who lived here back in the 1700s, so new settlers built their homes around it," Clark said as they started up the trail. "Access to fresh water was vital, and when the tough winters came, they could ice fish. But the settlement's long gone, except for a few bits of homesteads and some graves."

"Catastrophe?"

Clark's smile was thin and sad. "Like a lot of good ghost stories, it's always a tragedy. In this case, a young boy went missing in 1768. The men in the settlement, which had been named Harper's Row, all went out to look for him. The women stayed behind and checked cellars, sheds, even climbed trees to look for the little guy." They came around a bend in the trail that would lead up, and then down again. Closer to where Harper's Row had once flourished.

"Oh no."

"Unfortunately."

Jasper winced in a way that looked like it hurt. "Please don't tell me the boy was eaten by a bear or something."

"Worse. See, Harper's Row had taken up the prime real estate, so to speak, by the lake. This disgruntled another group of settlers nearby. Their settlement was rougher and relied on that lake more heavily for their cattle, and because they had found copper in the hills to the north. Mining of any kind takes water, and lots of it, and Harper's Row wanted a cut of the proceeds in return for access to the lake *and* their silence. Copper was incredibly valuable even then, and eventually whole towns were built up around copper mines in this area. But at the time, the boom was just getting started. And that's not to even get into white settlers stealing land from indigenous tribes and causing death and destruction."

Their boots crunching through forest detritus was the only sound for several long moments. "I had no idea. And I'm starting to understand why you think there may be a ghost trail at this spot."

Clark clicked his tongue. "Exactly. So, this other settlement, which didn't have a name, was finally so pissed off that they decided to exact a little revenge. One of the men, a guy named Daniel Truce – ironic, given what happened – saw the little boy wandering right before dusk. Truce was a bit of a muckraker and liked to stir things up, so when he saw this kid, he saw opportunity, too. Daniel snatched the kid up, thinking he'd ransom the boy for unfettered access to the lake. It went sideways, badly. The boy died."

By what little light there was left in the day, Clark could see Jasper was staring at the ground, hands balled up tight in his pockets. "That's horrible," Jasper said softly.

"I can move forward, if this is too much–"

Jasper shook his head. "These stories are always so sad. It's why I wanted to write about ghost trails, maybe discover some lost souls in the process and remind everyone of who they were. But keep going, please."

Jasper's little confession tugged hard on Clark's heartstrings. He was a sensitive soul, too. So out of sheer human empathy, he put his hand on Jasper's arm and squeezed. "All right. If you're sure."

"I am. Promise."

Clark waited a few moments as they trekked up a steep slope before continuing his story. "I've read different versions of how the boy died. Some say Truce killed him in a fit of rage, others wrote it was an accident. The boy's mother, Matilda, wrote in her journal that it looked like her boy had fallen or been pushed. His leg was broken, his skull split as if he'd crashed into a rock. But no matter what happened, we do know that Truce brought the boy back, because Matilda recognized the man's limp as he tried to run away from their house."

"He left the boy there?" Jasper asked.

Clark nodded. "According to Matilda, her son's body had been placed at their doorstep. It was the metaphorical straw that broke the camel's back. Matilda fired up the rest of Harper's Row against Truce and the other settlement, the men brought their guns..." Clark shook his head. "It was a bloodbath. Bodies on the ground, houses burned, livestock slaughtered. Those who survived buried the dead and left the area forever."

"Left the wilderness to reclaim it," Jasper said quietly. "I understand now. All that death would leave an indelible mark."

They stopped at the top of the hill and looked down. "From that band of pine trees to the west, all along the southern shore of the lake was Harper's Row," Clark said, his finger pointing out the spot. "We won't be the only ones here for sure, but I think we stand a good shot at seeing something. Maybe a remnant of a spirit, maybe a lost soul." He grinned up at Jasper. "Maybe a ghost trail."

Jasper was quiet for several long beats, gazing out over the darkening landscape. "Thank you. For caring," he finally said. "I knew it for certain after we talked at The Golden Unicorn, but I was hoping I wasn't wrong in thinking you understood. You know I've never actually *seen* a ghost trail? Every time I go out on a hunt, I hope I do."

Clark swallowed hard, felt the motion of his throat in stark relief against every other sensation clanging their way through his body. "But you've got reports of them, from dozens of people."

"I treat it a bit like alien sightings. I believe, but that belief isn't totally unshakeable. Not like it is for someone who has seen or experienced ghost trails. I write about ghost trails because of the *stories* that come out of those sightings. It's just my hope that one day, I'll have my own experience and feel less like a passive chronicler through the annals of time, and more like an active historian working to document something vital, something *real*."

"That's...rather sweet. I hadn't thought of it like that." Clark stared up at the sky and took a deep breath. Excitement was not a fire in his veins, but a steady simmer. It had been a long time since he'd had a sighting, but tonight felt different. Maybe the area, maybe the company. Either way, he couldn't wait to get started. "Shall we?"

Jasper grinned at him. "Let's go."

Chapter Nine

Elodie was either a saint or a deeply patient person. Bren couldn't find the right words to say on the ride back, so she let silence fill the car. The driver didn't seem to mind, either, which was a relief. Making small talk was far out of Bren's ability right now.

When the car stopped outside the rambling farmhouse she and Clark owned, Elodie quickly paid the driver. "You didn't have to do that," Bren said as they got out.

Elodie gave her a small smile. "Bren, you're right. I didn't have to do any of this. But I wanted to." She looked away, her mouth dipping into a frown. "Can we talk inside? It's kind of cold."

"Yeah. Yeah, of course." Bren led Elodie up the steps to the front door. The boards under their feet creaked and the screen door squeaked as she opened it. The sounds of the house – sounds she was so used to – seemed incredibly loud in the still night air. "Sorry about the mess," Bren said as they got inside. "It's been a busy week."

Bren turned to see Elodie taking in the house. A lot of their parents lingered in the worn furniture and thick rugs and faded paint. She and Clark could have easily sold the house, or done remodels, but it would have never felt right. And for all Bren and her twin got along now, they'd both been at their lowest after Mom had passed. Small things like moving lamps or changing curtains had turned into vicious arguments. Bren tried not to think about it even so many years later.

"It's wonderful," Elodie said. "Somehow exactly what I expected and yet not."

"How's that?"

Elodie pointed to the signed concert posters gracing the wall along the stairs to their right. "Those, for one."

"Those were Dad's. He *loved* live music. Said it was his church." Bren took their coats to the closet and let Elodie have some space to take off her shoes. On her way back, Bren paused at the foot of those stairs. From here, she could see into the living room with its big sandstone fireplace and mismatched armchairs. And if she looked down the hall, the kitchen sat at the end, waiting for someone to come and use the industrial stove or complain about the dripping faucet.

"Are you sure it's okay I'm here?" Elodie paused, chewed on her lip. "I don't want to intrude."

"Yeah, it is. I realize we don't know each other that well, Elodie, but I don't say things I don't mean."

Elodie brightened. "Okay, good. Cause I thought as much but I didn't want to assume anything."

Bren blew out a breath. She should probably just tell Elodie what happened, so the woman (the one Bren might be a smidge attracted to, surely that didn't calculate into this) didn't think Bren was flighty or foolhardy. "Want some tea? We'll get the good stuff, Clark won't care."

"Sure. But let me help."

"All right."

Bren set Elodie to work with filling the kettle while she pulled out Clark's neatly organized tray of tea. Every year for his birthday, Bren bought her brother a new jar – some find from a flea market or yard sale. He preferred clay or ceramic jars, the older the better, and would take the time to clean them before adding in his favorite loose-leaf teas. Over the years, the tray filled up and now Clark was fully stocked with everything from green teas smelling of rain-soaked woods to black teas dotted with rose buds that looked like little pink jewels.

Bren gave Elodie the tea tray, pointing out a few favorites. "This one's nice," she said, hand hovering over a pot of cinnamon tea. "Or this one, it has pomegranate in it."

"You pick." Elodie smiled at her. "I trust you."

"All right."

Elodie backed up a step, turning her attention to the kettle on the stove. The woman was clearly trying to not hem Bren in, but in some way she welcomed Elodie's warmth, her scent. Elodie being easy to talk to was one thing – some people exuded that energy – but something about her made Bren want to open up completely.

Maybe she was tired of being alone.

Maybe instead of giving thin smiles and leaving half-moon indents in her palms when in groups of strangers, she could learn to do more than *deal with it*. Clark thought Bren was so sure of herself all the time, but there was a reason she kept her apartment above the barn, and a reason she slept alone.

Maybe Elodie could be a friend. But to even dream about making that happen, Bren needed to remember what it was like to be a part of someone else's life. She'd spent so much time hidden away after the accident. But in those darker days, Bren had taken her therapist's advice and really examined her past. And, it turned out, he was right: she stayed away from everyone to avoid pain. She made connections sparingly and barely talked to anyone outside the greenhouse employees and Clark. She had little in the way of a social life. Dating was a distant thought.

She was lonely and sad and thought she had to spend the rest of her life squirreled away in the shadows, so she didn't inflict her pain on anyone else.

No more.

Bren had slowly been inching her way toward that decision but now, standing in the kitchen of her parents' house – now her and Clark's – with someone who seemed to care? The chance to leap was right in front of her. If she never took it, she'd never find out.

"Chamomile," Bren said, an air of decisiveness in her voice to cover up her nerves. "We grew the flower in the greenhouse, and Clark really got into blending his own teas a few years ago. I wish he'd let me sell this one, customers would go crazy."

"You two are close." Bren turned to see Elodie with her back against the counter, a softly pensive look on her cherubic face. "I feel like I've seen him around the greenhouse."

"Yeah. During the busiest days, he'll pitch in when he can." Bren brushed a hand over her hair. "We're twins, so he's got this hair and the family nose. But we've always been there for each other."

When she looked away to begin preparing their cups, Bren could still feel Elodie's gaze on her. It was nice to not feel rushed or pressured to talk. Part of Bren wanted to ask if Elodie would rather go over to her apartment, but the woman seemed perfectly at home in the haphazard, cozy farmhouse. She *fit*, even in that glittering champagne jumpsuit, looking all the more like a model rather than the clumsy woman who dumped water on Bren's head and loved plants and folklore. Bren liked that such a contrast could exist in the same person. It was a good reminder that most folks had multitudes.

"I admit I'm a little jealous," Elodie replied as the kettle began to whistle. "I'm an only child and my parents were always so busy."

"Latchkey kid?"

"Oh, definitely. But I got to read and wander outside, so it worked out in the end."

While their tea steeped, Bren led Elodie over to the little kitchen table. "Sorry," she said, sweeping up the small pile of junk mail Clark never seemed to throw into the recycling bin. "Clark's out on a weekend trip and I haven't been able to clean some things up yet."

"Bren." Suddenly Elodie was there, with her soft blond and pink wavy hair and big doe eyes and gentle frown. Worried, not disapproving. "You're fine. It's your house. And it's nice being in spaces where people actually *live*." She waved a hand over the kitchen. "Besides, you should see my place. I got this bright idea to reorganize my closets and uh..."

Bren laughed. "Disaster? It would be for sure if I did that."

"Oh, total disaster." Elodie laughed with her and like *that*, the tension popped. A mere soap bubble now faded to a distant memory. "I wind up thinking of all these great ways to label things and put them in cute little bins and then I uh...get very distracted. By a shirt I forgot I had and then I'm trying it on to see if it still fits." Elodie sighed and put her chin in her hand, leaning into the fragrant steam from her cup. "Okay, that smells amazing."

"It should be done." Bren pulled the strainers out and set them aside before Elodie lifted the cup to her nose and inhaled, then gingerly sipped her tea. "Good?"

"Oh my god. *Incredible*." Elodie took another sip, not seeming to mind what must have been scalding tea. "Holy shit. I want to marry this. You don't even know."

Bren let out a snort. It was nice, watching someone appreciate her and her brother's handiwork. Plants were easy people-pleasers most of the time, but something more intensive like tea blending took real dedication. Bren kept her plants and let Clark be the experimenter; the one who would dive into his books and video tutorials to learn a new thing, then try it out. Bren used to get jealous at how quickly new skills came to him, but over time, understood her place in the world with a new appreciation.

Plants made sense. They sprouted, lived, died. Sometimes they only needed a bit of sunlight and water and they flourished. Others were finicky and it took patience to see them through the rough spots full of yellowing leaves and moldy soil, too much water or not enough humidity. And occasionally they weren't meant for this world, no matter how much care and devotion you put into them. That was okay, too.

"Hey, Bren?"

"Hmmm?" Bren looked up from her cup and into soft eyes that asked for nothing but honesty.

"Are you okay? You don't have to talk about what happened, but you got this kind of far-away look." Elodie's smile was as soft as her eyes, but what shocked Bren to her core was when Elodie put her hand, palm up, on the table. Right between them. An open invitation.

Few people looked at Bren like that. She was the stoic survivor, the fighter who bore everything and asked for nothing in return. An ex used to say that, in the multiverse, every version of Bren was the same because even the endless paths of time needed reliable sorts. Their words had hurt – then, and now.

Elodie looked at her like Bren had value outside of what she could handle. Outside of *reliable* and *stalwart*. That she wasn't simply what she could bear.

"Honestly, no. I've been feeling kind of…" Bren paused, chewing on her gristle-like thoughts. "Adrift, I suppose. I've been trying to go on every day like everything's normal. And I have nothing to complain about. The business is successful, we can pay our bills and have food and a roof over our heads. Everything is *fine*. We're so fucking lucky." Something lodged in her throat, some unspoken truth that even Bren hadn't wanted to acknowledge.

Not when she woke up at three in the morning and couldn't fall back asleep.

Not when she worked from open to close to keep from staring aimlessly at her apartment walls.

Not even to Clark or her therapist or Iris.

And the thing she ran from wasn't *always* the goddamn mushroom wall incident or the months she spent holed up in the greenhouse afterwards. Sometimes, Bren felt like she was simply running from her own mind.

Elodie's brow was creased but her gaze stayed soft. Hell, Elodie herself looked soft, glowing in the light from old yellow bulbs in a fixture several decades out of date, all frosted glass and bronze trim. "Bren?"

Bren leaned forward, tugged by the invisible cord that was the woman seated in front of her. It spilled out; vicious, ugly truth, dumped right into the lap of someone unsuspecting. "I have clinical depression. And about eighteen months ago, a video of me saving one of my staff from an accident went viral. I really, really fought to keep everything the same, but these cameras and people kept showing up. It was horrible. I don't like attention and this was like having a thousand spotlights on me. I couldn't breathe most days. And there were a lot of nights I thought about being done. Really done, you know. Not my first go-round with those thoughts but the accident and the video made it...amplified somehow." Bren let out a deep breath, the knot long formed in her chest as tight as it had ever been. "I'm just getting back to things. Clearly I'm still working on that, given what happened tonight. I'm really sorry for that."

Those eyes were staring at her, right into her fucking soul. Elodie's hand was still on the table. A silent offer. One Bren wasn't sure if she could take. "I understand. I do," Elodie said quietly, her gaze never wavering. "Please know, if nothing else, I would never judge you for anything and you have nothing to apologize for. I promise."

Bren licked her lips, flinching at their dryness. "You might be too kind for your own good."

That got her a snort. "Hardly. Did I ever tell you why I came to Alpine University?" When Bren shook her head, Elodie actually chuckled. "Suffice to say I don't like dishonest people and because I pissed off the wrong person, I got shit-canned. Dishonest people make me so angry." With care, Elodie put her hand on top of Bren's and Bren found she didn't want to move her own away. "You are not dishonest. You're forthright, which I happen to like. A lot."

Oh god, Bren thought. *Not this. Not...not hope. Not that flighty thing that seems to get ripped away so often.* "What does that mean?"

"If you want to hear the whole sordid story about my last employer, I'd love to tell you. Over dinner."

Chapter Ten

Clark thought of himself as a stickler only in terms of his job. Everything in order according to library organizational systems. When he left his job for the day, home was the more relaxed, comfortable place where it was okay to leave a few books on the table or make a stack of mail to take to the recycling bin. Sometimes he looked around the old farmhouse and got ideas on making it a bit more organized – seeing reels on social media featuring neatly labeled bins and baskets in a kitchen pantry, for example, might make Clark linger on what could be. But half the fun of every day was letting things come as they might. If things got a tad messy, that was okay.

But standing on the slight rise above where Harper's Row had been and seeing at least a dozen little circles of lights from flashlight bulbs made Clark's heart sink. He had kind of wanted this to be *his spot*. A few people around, sure, but there was no way any sightings would occur with so much raucous *life* hanging about.

The people below had practically turned the edge of the lake into a party, complete with...holy shit, someone was starting a bonfire. Not a small campfire, a massive thing that would send light out like a flare. That was against ghost hunter code and just good common sense. No spirit would come to such a place.

"I have no idea what's happening," he said, voice tinged with disappointment as he and Jasper stared down at the gathering. "The rules of the hunts are very clear. No large gatherings, no big fires. Plus, what if the fire gets out of control? I doubt anyone down there brought an extinguisher or even has a bucket of sand!" Clark whirled, ready to stomp back down to the main campsite and report what was going on.

A gentle hand on his arm stopped Clark in his tracks. "I know you're disappointed, Clark," Jasper said softly, staring down at Clark with kind eyes. "But we can find another spot."

The words left him immediately. "I wanted this to be perfect," Clark said, swallowing hard.

He had wanted all of this to be a perfect little ghost hunt in the woods, all alone with the man he'd been crushing on for months. And if something ghostly and exciting happened, he would be able to share it with Jasper. Someone who seemed a bit like him, who trusted but walked forward with eyes open. Clark hadn't met many people who could fully do both and remain steadfast to their ideals. He could trust in the organization of his job, the slight messiness of his home; in the scent of an old book to conjure up memories and the photos of his parents to provide solace when he was upset. And he could trust that spirits were real and occasionally sought out the living.

And if nothing exciting happened tonight and Clark got to stay close to Jasper? Well, that was exciting and a bit messy and yet perfect, too. Maybe he'd lean in at the same time Jasper would as they listened to the night fold in around them. Maybe they'd kiss. Maybe Jasper would put his hand on Clark's cheek and deepen the touch, make him shiver with want.

All of that rushed out of Clark's head now as he fumed. "I wanted this to be perfect," he repeated as he stared up at Jasper, feeling more solid in his convictions. "I wanted to share something with you."

"Clark." Jasper squeezed his arm and then let go. "You already have. You didn't have to invite me out here or share what you knew about Harper's Row. We could have sat in the pines all night, silent as the grave. Strangers who happened to be in the same spot at the same time."

Something knotted in Clark's chest. Jasper was close. Too close. Not close enough. "So now what?"

"We find our own spot. The perfect one." Jasper sniffed in the direction of the campers below. "Away from the ones who clearly aren't respecting why everyone else is out here."

Clark nodded, letting Jasper lead them west instead of north, away from the chaos and back into the safety of the night and the forest. As they walked, Clark consulted his notes once more. He had a backup site they could go to, closer to the settlement that had warred with Harper's Row. He shoved his disappointment away to focus, peering down at his phone screen.

"Thoughts?"

Clark glanced up at Jasper and nodded. "There should be a trail-head here. Cardinal Path. If we follow that west, we'll come to where historians think the other settlement had been. It's a bit of a walk but we're still ahead of schedule."

"Schedule?" Jasper looked amused. "There's a schedule?" His tone was gently teasing, not cruel in the least.

"Well," Clark replied, shifting his weight under such close scrutiny. "I mean, I had things kind of lined up. But those...camp wreckers threw me off. So, we still have time to get set up before real darkness falls."

Jasper waved a hand in the air. "Seems pretty dark to me."

"No, I mean..." Clark sighed and scrubbed a hand over his face. "Real darkness meaning the times when the veil between worlds is thin. Thin enough that something might get curious and wander over."

"I like that. It's beautiful, in its way."

"Yeah, I think so, too." Something stretched between them and it helped chase away Clark's disappointment. Maybe they could get back on track after all.

"Now that's a view."

Clark smiled, pleased with the bit of awe in Jasper's voice. He was right; the view was spectacular, even if they were a little further to the west than Clark had planned. Which was fine. Really. Because the rush of night sky felt bigger somehow, as if he could reach up and touch it with his fingertips. "Seconded. Wow, you can even see the moon from here."

Jasper set his pack down near a fallen log before putting a boot on the wood. "Seems sturdy," he said before sitting down. "So, you're the expert. How do you want to get started?"

Clark let out a silent sigh of relief. He had his ghost hunting routine down, and with two of them, it would go easier. "Start a small fire, get out my gear, and wait." He gave Jasper a sheepish smile. "There's more to it, of course, but this is a test of patience more than anything."

"Not one of belief?"

Clark pulled out his firestarter and lighter, then his waterproof kit as he replied. Jasper was *very* intuitive and just a bit intimidating in the moment, looking at Clark like he could see through him. "If you didn't believe, you wouldn't be out here with me."

"And just when I think you've got a lovely philosophical discussion for me, you punt one through, right here." Jasper held a closed fist against his heart. "I like how you surprise me."

Clark forced his hands not to shake as he built a small fire pit. Doing that took all his focus, so he stayed quiet while Jasper helped him pull rocks into a circle and gather up dry brush. They managed to get a fire going right as the the wind swept in, carrying with it the scent of rain. They were very likely getting drenched at some point tonight.

Fire now roaring, Clark gave Jasper instructions on how to place four white candles around the fire – one each at a cardinal direction. "Extra light, of course, but also a kind of welcome mat for spirits. So they know this is a space that doesn't seek to trap or use them. I could buy into the whole drawing runes in the dirt thing, but that always felt cheap."

"Cheap to use symbols of a philosophy you don't perhaps subscribe to?" Jasper asked as he slowly, carefully followed Clark's directions.

"Yeah. I didn't just yank this from a book, either." Clark smiled as he thought about Havaa and Pierre. It had been a bit since he'd seen either of them, though they texted in a group chat with he and Bren all the time. "I've got friends who are pagans and over the years they've found their path in their practices and been willing to share. As long as we're respectful and don't do anything advantageous or harmful, we're abiding by their laws."

Jasper placed the last candle, lit it, and then came to sit beside Clark. "I'm grateful to you and your friends for sharing what you know," he said quietly as they watched the candles and fire flicker in the wind.

"I'm already learning a lot more than I expected. But I shouldn't be surprised, with the company I'm lucky enough to have tonight."

Oh gods, he was *close* again and Clark wanted so badly to lean into Jasper's warmth. *Yearning* burned in him. Clark felt pulled in two directions – toward his goal, and toward the man beside him.

Focus. You're here for a reason. Maybe there will be a chance later for something more. Focus.

And then again, maybe Jasper was a mind reader. "Can I..." Jasper shook his head and Clark watched a tendril of blond hair fall into his eyes.

Heart thumping hard in his chest, Clark said, "Can you what?"

Jasper's smile was soft, almost shy. He didn't quite meet Clark's eyes when he replied, "I thought about doing that cheesy thing where I offer to put my arm around you, to keep us both warm. Silly, I know."

This is happening. Okay, okay, don't panic. It's just an arm. Fuck, why do I feel like a clumsy teenager again? Thank god the acne disappeared years ago. "Ask. You might be surprised by my answer."

Jasper's smile curled, now delighted but still soft. Satisfied. "Oh. Right. Ahem." He straightened, pulled his shoulders back, and now met Clark's gaze head-on. "It's cold. Maybe, while we wait, we could keep each other warm?"

Clark fought not to grin. He wanted to play along, after all. "What did you have in mind?"

The moment Clark's words left him, Jasper's teasing little smile turned *interested*.

As if he was thinking about more than offering an arm to drape over Clark's shoulders.

"Well, seeing as how we're on the watch for spirits and ghost trails, let's start with this?" Jasper slowly, carefully placed his arm around Clark, the weight of it heavy but comforting. Clark's will evaporated and he leaned in, entranced by how Jasper was looking at him with keen expectation.

"We can start there," Clark replied, smiling up at Jasper. The wind tousled a bit more hair from the edges of Jasper's knit cap, so Clark brushed a bit of it off Jasper's cold cheek. "If I can do that."

The sound of Jasper swallowing hard hit Clark square in the gut. "You can."

"Good. I'm glad." Clark turned back to the fire and the candles, finally able to focus now that Jasper and his warmth were close. Funny, he would have thought them distracting but the *temptation* of them had been the true reason for his loss of focus. Now he could stare at the flames and *hope*.

He'd never, ever lacked for belief that spirits hovered on the edges of some unseen realm. Clark had seen a few strange things over the course of nights just like this. But he'd always been alone, or close to it if he'd gone to an event where campers stayed in an area instead of spreading out. Having someone close was special in an odd kind of way. But he was glad it was Jasper, someone who believed. Someone who never made him feel silly or superstitious.

The flicker of fire drew Clark in. As his body relaxed, he could feel his mind open; slowly, at first, like a rusty crank. The woods, the quiet, the warmth beside him were catalysts. He'd always firmly believed that he was more sensitive than most, and that made Clark feel like he was part of something bigger.

"I've never been a religious person," Clark said quietly as they stared into the fire. "But I've always felt like there was something pulling on me. Even when I was a kid. My dad called me 'attuned' and he and my mom let me explore to the limits of my understanding. I'd check out books on religions and ghosts and beg them to buy me a Ouija board." Clark paused to look down at his boots and mush his thoughts together into some semblance of meaning.

Jasper's arm tightened around him. "You don't have to share anything you don't want to."

"I know. I do. But it's actually nice to be able to do this. It makes me feel less alone." Clark looked up at Jasper and saw nothing but open acceptance. Somewhere near his heart, an old wound was finally being stitched up.

Jasper squeezed Clark's shoulder, his fingers strong and comforting as they pressed down. "I imagine we all need to share some of those parts of ourselves. No one's a vault."

"No one healthy, anyways," Clark replied, making Jasper chuckle. "And you actually listen, which is nice. I've had those run-ins with people who think they need to, I don't know, convert me or something. It's gross and intrusive and makes everything about them. I even went to a 'spiritual sharing circle' once and that was very much not good."

"How so?"

Clark shuddered at the memory of stale scones and weak coffee mixed with the scent of old cigarettes. But that was all jumbled up with memories of the people – their scrutinizing glares, disapproving frowns, the rosary one woman wore wrapped around her wrist and how it clacked with every nervous twitch. "I thought it would actually be a chance to share. But everyone was so damn judgey. Even the supposedly spiritual people who hang witch lanterns and burn sage. They were all so wary of each other, and that made everyone jumpy. I thought it was going to be a chance to meet other people, see how they perceived the world. It was kind of sad."

Jasper stayed silent for a long moment, finally saying, "Did you go back?"

"No, it wasn't worth it. And we – my sister and I – started playing board games with friends on that night. Better worth my time, I think." He peered up at Jasper, curiosity gnawing at him. "What about you? Why ghost trails? I know we talked a little bit about it, and if you don't want to share, that's totally fine..."

"Clark."

"Yeah?"

"Did you see that?"

Clark froze as he tried to tune into their surroundings. Jasper's arm around him felt heavier than before. Even the air had a weight to it, the cold a knife through his layers. As he and Jasper stared at the fire, the eastern candle sputtered out.

"What did you see?" Clark whispered, trying to track Jasper's gaze. Jasper was staring out into the tree line, eyes wide and his lips parted.

"I'm..." Jasper shook his head, then pulled off his hat and dropped it into his lap. "I'm not sure. Ghost trails are supposed to be white or green-ish energy, like shimmering lines. Hard to spot unless you're really looking." Jasper swallowed hard and slowly pulled his arm away to point east. "But I swore I saw something kind of glittering just over there. Like a small bit of light. I thought it was a flashlight at first but as soon as I looked at it head-on, it disappeared."

Clark was immediately on his feet and motioning for Jasper to stand. Excitement was a drumbeat in his veins, fueling that sense he always had that there was *something* just on the other side. "Come on," he said as he scooped up the eastern candle and started to put out all the other fires. "We've got a trail to follow. This candle will help us."

Jasper still wore that slight expression of disbelief, but he didn't hesitate to follow Clark from their makeshift camp and into the woods. "Stay close to me?" he asked.

Clark grinned. "Of course."

Chapter Eleven

An hour later, Bren and Elodie were sharing plates of greasy eggs, turkey sausage, biscuits, and little bowls of fruit across a worn diner table. "Statler's All-Night" was a local gem; the kind of place you went to after a night of bar-hopping, or early in the morning before hitting the road on a long drive, and it was the place you took out-of-town family and friends. The coffee was night-sky black and would easily wake the dead, and the faux blue leather booths were cracked from years and years of customers. It was also the kind of place where their outfits wouldn't get any strange looks; for all everyone else in Statler's knew, Bren and Elodie were just on their way out, or on their way back in. It was funny to Bren how both of those were technically true.

"I like your taste in dinner dates," Elodie said as a blue-aproned member of the wait staff brought over more water and coffee. "I'm going to be buzzing all night from the coffee. And the company."

"How do you do that?" Bren watched as Elodie glanced up with a quicksilver grin. "Make it look so easy."

Elodie shrugged. "What? Giving you a compliment?"

"Well, when you put it like that. Yeah."

"Bren, it's not hard when it's honest. Remember what I said about dishonest people?" When Bren nodded, Elodie took a sip of water and cast her gaze about the diner, as if gathering her thoughts. "I like you. You know who you are, and if I had to guess, you're pretty aware of your faults and your good spots. That's rare." Bren gave her a skeptical look. "I'm serious! Do you know how many people lack self-awareness? It's staggering. And the bummer is once you realize it, you can't help but notice. The next time you're in a crowded place, watch how many people stop in the middle of traffic, or a doorway."

"That's just rudeness," Bren said.

Elodie stabbed a strawberry half onto her fork and waved it around as she talked. Bren was utterly charmed. "Yes, and oftentimes, a total lack of awareness of the space their own body occupies. A plus B can equal C in those instances, too. But we're also really good at tricking ourselves into thinking we're the only one who matters, and not always in that selfish kind of way. I just mean that we're often so wrapped up in our own thoughts and feelings that we forget about the world, and the people around us."

Elodie popped the strawberry piece into her mouth with a grin, leaving Bren to gape at her before clearing her throat to say, "Weird. From the way you talk, I'd think you study human nature or something. Maybe through stories. Are you a folklorist, perhaps?"

That got Bren a laugh before Elodie replied. "Our deepest fears and smallest worries go into stories. But even the ones about people simply existing have something to share. And speaking of sharing...I have a confession."

Strange. With anyone else save Clark, those words would have sent Bren's stomach plummeting, like when, on a school trip, she'd looked down from the Empire State Building and felt dizzy and sick. But this wasn't like that. "Okay."

"Bren, you shared something really personal with me earlier tonight. And I wanted you to know what that meant. All this?" Elodie's rings flashed as she waved a hand at the diner. "Not maybe the most romantic date spot ever, but it's real. I *wanted* something real, something comfortable. And I don't know what commercial viral thing happened, but I'm not about to go look it up. I don't care about that. I like *you*."

Those words came to Bren like that sensation of walking on wet sand and getting nowhere fast. She heard them, but the more she tried to process, all that got stuck in Bren's mind was *date don't know commercial like you*. "I don't understand," Bren replied slowly.

"Shit, I'm so sorry! I just blurted all that out and it really should have been timed better –"

"No, I mean...really?" Bren leaned forward, her palms flat on the table as she scrutinized Elodie's pretty face. "You don't know the commercial?"

Elodie didn't seem at all perturbed with how Bren stared at her. "No idea. I don't watch viral videos or anything on social media. Haven't been on there since I was fired from my last university. And if I saw anything around the time whatever happened, well, happened, it would have been in passing over the story on a news site. I swear, Bren, I've got no clue what you're talking about and I don't want to know more than what you tell me. It's not who you are, it's something that *happened* to you."

There was a telltale hitch in her breathing now, one that would have sent Clark bolting for the tissue box. But instead, in a diner on South Street, under the color change of a stoplight and with only napkins at her disposal, Bren began to cry.

"Oh god, I am *so sorry*." Elodie was immediately at her side, sliding into the booth and pressing her warmth into Bren, filling her head with the scent of sugar and apples. "Here, here, take these napkins and I'll get some more –"

"Elodie?"

"Yeah?"

Bren sniffled and wiped her eyes, grateful Iris had given her waterproof mascara. It had seemed so pointless mere hours ago. "Please don't apologize."

Elodie rubbed Bren's arm. "I didn't mean to make you cry."

"No, it's a good thing. Trust me." Bren blinked away more tears, and through them, saw Elodie wave down a wait staff member. "I don't cry easily. Sometimes I wish I did."

Elodie handed her a pile of napkins from the wait staff and took some for herself, dabbing at her eyes. "And I cry at everything. What a pair we make."

"I'm not mad at it," Bren replied with a small smile. "Contrasts can be nice. Good, even."

Something shifted on Elodie's face then. Something small but important. Through her tears, she said, "Opposites do tend to attract, as the adage goes."

With Elodie acknowledging what she was hedging at, Bren felt brave enough to *try*. Just a little. She reached out and Elodie met her halfway, tangling their fingers together on top of the cracked and worn tabletop. The sound of the other customers and the scent of coffee and grease faded away and all that was left was *her* and *them*. "I'm really not good at this kind of thing," Bren said softly, unable to tear her eyes away from the sight of their joined hands.

"Neither am I." Elodie pressed her shoulder into Bren's. "Maybe we can figure it out together."

They left the diner soon after. The air between them had changed, but instead of some kind of electrical charge, it felt comfortable. Elodie had slipped her hand into Bren's as they walked down the street, their feet carrying them with no real aim or purpose. But Bren was certain neither one of them wanted to go home quite yet.

"I was thinking about plant folklore the other day. For the podcast," Elodie said as they walked, their boots crunching over the remnants of winter salt and sludge on the sidewalk. "And I realized that it might be fun to start with the things people know, or think they do. Lavender, clover, thyme, rosemary, things like that. Do you think that might work after we record the Q&A? I know you and Iris are leaving it up to me, and I appreciate that so much. But I don't want to lead your listeners down a path they're not interested in. I'm sure you know a lot of that information already, so I hope it doesn't bore you."

Bren gave Elodie's hand a tug, bringing the other woman close. Elodie went willingly, a puzzled smile on her face. "You talking about plants is endlessly fascinating," Bren breathed, her words little wisps of cloud on the chill night air. "And I think *you're* endlessly fascinating. I want to know more."

"I never did tell you about my shitty old job and why I left."

"That's a good start. But I want to know more. Anything you'll share with me." Bren looked down at Elodie, having long decided to go all in but hadn't quite walked up to this line. Until now. "I'd really like to kiss you right now. If that's okay."

"Please."

One word. One little word on a breathy gasp and something in Bren broke. Elodie grabbed her by the coat lapels just as Bren angled her head. They met in the middle in spectacular fashion, Elodie's mouth the perfect slant against her own. When Bren touched Elodie's face, a whisper of fingers against her cheek, Elodie sighed.

It was perfect. Too short by many, many seconds. But it was a beautifully good start.

"That happened," Elodie said, her bi-colored eyes half-lidded, her voice thick. "Oh, that happened. Wow."

Bren stifled her laugh. She felt lightheaded and so sure at the same time. It was a twin-edged blade of sensation, melding into soft warmth as they stared at each other. "You are something else," she whispered, letting her fingers dance over Elodie's warm cheek once more. "I feel very lucky right now."

"Lucky?" Elodie had a dazed tone to her voice, like she'd woken up from a long nap.

"Yeah. Because you haven't run screaming in the other direction and I want to do that again."

"Oh, Bren."

Bren was pulled into another kiss, and this one bore the blunt-edged teeth of desire. No full-on bite quite yet, but the promise was there. That promise made Bren grip Elodie harder this time, using her height and strength to haul them against the brick wall of a nearby shop. Thoughts of lifting Elodie by the waist were pushed away for now, but it was tempting. That nagging knowledge that they were on a very public street at a not indecent hour also kept Bren's baser wants at bay, but only just.

She could taste Elodie now - apples and sugar, yes, but something darker sat there, too. A promise like caramel on the tongue. Bren kept her hands at Elodie's waist, never moving up or down, hoping the other woman *understood*.

I won't press, but I want this. Want you.

They finally separated and Elodie's breath churned in the space between them. "You are way, way too good at that," Elodie said, voice hoarse now. "Bren."

With the back of her hand, Bren brushed the hair out of Elodie's eyes. "Let me make you dinner. A proper date. I want to."

Elodie's nod was quick and that little movement set Bren's heart thumping harder. "Yes. I'd love that. Anytime, seriously. I'll bring wine and all my good stories."

"All of them? Such a promise."

"You're feeding me. I'm liable to never leave." Elodie batted her eyelashes at Bren, the gold shadow on her eyelids entrancing in the streetlight overhead. "I'm an easy date."

"So am I. I just don't do much of it. Dating." Bren didn't want this night, this golden hour, to end, but a date – a real one – made the future seem so much brighter.

Elodie took Bren's chin between her thumb and forefinger, hauling her down once more. "Their loss. Looks like you're mine, now."

The next night

"Okay, so I'm an easy date, and a quick one," Elodie said as Bren opened the door to her apartment. "I'm early! Sorry."

"Don't be." Like Bren was going to be upset that the person she'd been aching to see all day was at her door fifteen minutes early. "But now you have to help peel carrots."

"Oh *noooo*," Elodie said, laughing. "The dreaded carrots. However will I survive?"

Bren waved her in, taking the proffered bottle of wine and holding out her hand for Elodie's coat and bags. Elodie kept her tote bag close, though. "It's a surprise," she said, a sly smile on her face. "For after dinner."

"Keep your secrets, then," Bren teased before leading Elodie to the kitchen. With her apartment being one big, open space save the bedroom and bathroom, Bren always felt like guests were more at ease. No bumping down dark hallways or stumbling into doorways looking for the toilet, and no question about how to move around each other when there was plenty of room to maneuver. It was the same kind of courtesy she had set up at Pennyroyal & Mugwort, but admittedly strange in a business that was usually all crowded shelves and uneven walkways between rickety racks of pots. Why shove yourself through spaces when you could move with ease? That had never made any sense to Bren.

So, to watch Elodie move through the apartment – *her space* – and smile and run her fingers over smooth countertops and across the backs of soft velvet chairs? It made something in Bren shift in delight. Maybe it was odd, but for her, it felt good to have someone enjoy the space like she did.

And just like she'd adapted instantly to Bren's place, Elodie smoothly slid into food prep mode. While she peeled carrots, Bren chopped onions and potatoes. "It's a chicken barley soup," Bren explained as she watched curls of orange hit the counter. "Old family recipe. I figured it would be nice, with how chilly it's been."

"I love it and I immediately want it in my mouth," Elodie said. "And I already spied the rolls in the oven, so I'm prepared for a food coma afterwards."

"I don't know if it's food coma worthy," Bren replied.

"Oh, it definitely is. I have no doubt." Elodie reached for another carrot, peering at it before taking the peeler to it. "Did you grow these?"

Bren flushed. "Maybe."

"Damn. Gorgeous and smart and good with her hands and able to grow beautiful carrots." Elodie set the carrot down and pinned Bren with a heated look. "I put that down so this didn't turn into some weird penis euphemism."

Bren had to set her knife down so she didn't cut herself because she was laughing too hard.

"So, here's the story," Elodie said as the soup simmered and the yeasty smell of homemade rolls filled the apartment. They'd decided to sit on Bren's couch so Bren could keep an eye on the soup, or so she proclaimed. Bren wasn't sure if Elodie had other motives for sitting on the low-slung couch versus the stools around the small kitchen island, but Bren couldn't ignore how close Elodie was. Her warmth, her scent, the way her dark navy sweater shifted a little so the top of Elodie's shoulder was exposed. It made Bren was to put her lips to that skin and see if she tasted as good as she smelled.

"I'm mentally preparing myself," Bren said with an internal shake to her libido.

"Hah, well, it's not *that* scandalous. But I was an assistant professor at Great Lakes University, up in Wisconsin, for four years. My first big job in academia." Elodie sipped her wine, leaving Bren to watch Elodie's face closely. The last thing Bren wanted was for Elodie to be uncomfortable. "I was just a general English professor, and my students were mostly okay. However, the faculty sucked, and the job paid fucking *nothing*. So as excited as I was to have my first real job tangentially related to what I really wanted to study, it made things tough. Long hours, students needing more help than I could reasonably give, and I was broke."

"I'm so sorry," Bren said on instinct. "I've heard those jobs are essentially unpaid internships."

"Yeah, basically. So, everyone there at that level worked another job. Had to, to survive. So, I took what I could find – food delivery on the weekends, extra tutoring sessions. And then Sylvie, another assistant prof about my age but in mathematics, hooked me up with a bartending gig."

Elodie paused to drain her wine and Bren instantly put her hand out. "Another?"

"Nah, but thank you for offering." Elodie set the glass on a coaster on the side table. "I've largely lost my taste for it past one glass every now and then. It uh...leads to bad decisions on my part."

Bren nodded. "I get it. I'm not huge on it either. Losing control is a fear I've always had."

Elodie shivered. "And hangovers. Horrible."

"Agreed."

With fluid ease, Elodie shifted to lean back against the couch, her bi-colored gaze gone serious as quickly as her smile had disappeared. It was as if Bren could see the gears shifting.

"So, here's the fun part. And I say that because I know you won't judge me. I was working until close one night at the bar, and this place is pretty queer friendly, so you know, sometimes folks ask you out. No one was pushy, thank god, but it can get uncomfortable. But this woman who I'd seen there a fair bit was lingering, kind of hanging out at the bar. She orders one more at last call, I pour it. Gin and tonic, I'll never forget that."

The air felt heavy now as Elodie paused again and Bren could just tell this was not going to be a story that ended well. Heart in her throat, she put her hand beside the couch, close to Elodie but not on her. Elodie looked down, smiled softly, and put her hand on top of Bren's. "And she was pretty, Bren. Short blond hair in kind of a razor-edged pixie cut, long eyelashes, purple lipstick. So, when she's looking at me like the night's just getting started and well...we wind up at my shitty apartment a few blocks up the street. Suffice it to say we carry on like that for a bit. Nothing serious, just fun." Elodie shot Bren a sad look. "I'm guessing you're already trying to figure out whose wife she was."

"Ah, shit," Bren said quietly.

"Yep. I had no idea she was married, let alone to the head of my department. I had no idea I was her little play toy on the side, or that she'd use me to get back at her crappy husband." Elodie shrugged as if to say *the past is the past and I'm fine*, but Bren could see how badly this bothered her. How could it not?

"How did you find out?" Bren asked after a moment. "Did the husband find you?"

Elodie let out a dry laugh. "Yeah, a few months later. Apparently they'd gotten in a fight earlier in the evening, because she shows up to the bar with him in tow, making snide remarks about how she's been getting better from her side piece than he has with his."

Bren was gobsmacked. "What?"

"Yeah! Points right at me and starts talking about what *good care* I take care of her," Elodie said, venom in her voice now. "How she should have never married a man who didn't know how to use his tongue properly."

Under Elodie's soft palm, Bren balled her hand into a fist. "The fucking nerve..."

Elodie's gaze went distant for a moment, as if the memory still had a hold on her. "Yeah so to make a long story short, this all gets around campus. I get handed an ultimatum: take a demotion or leave. I quit.

The head of the department – *the husband* – was never going to let me have a moment's peace if I stayed. So, I packed my shit up and lived with my Aunt Becky in Minnesota for a bit and applied everywhere. But I finally got lucky with Alpine U. And you know, they actually seem to care about their staff. I have a small stipend to help with my research project. So, things turned out all right."

"More than all right, maybe," Bren said, hedging on a bet she was terrified to take. "It brought you here. I got to meet you. I feel lucky in that, in a very selfish way. But I'm so sorry that all happened. What a bunch of assholes."

Elodie drew closer then, all the righteous fury in her face gone, replaced with that softness that made Bren want to fall into her. "Thank you," Elodie said, squeezing Bren's hand again. "It sucks. It did and it still does. And it definitely made me wary of any kind of romantic entanglements." She reached up to gently brush her fingertips over Bren's dark hair, where it fell over her shoulder. Bren had kept her wardrobe simple in the name of cooking hazards, but Elodie never made her feel underdressed. It was a strange sensation, as if Bren was *enough*.

So, with all that swirling in her head, Bren leaned forward as Elodie did. She heard Elodie sigh, felt her breath ghost over her lips, and sank into their kiss like it was the most natural thing in the world.

"I like it better here," Elodie murmured against Bren's lips a moment later. "I think we're going to be good for each other.

Chapter Twelve

Traipsing through the woods with only two flashlights might have felt like a mistake. But Clark held firm to Jasper's arm as they forged ahead, purpose driving them toward the exciting and unknown. In the darkest part of the wood, Clark might have felt lost or even a little apprehensive, but Jasper was *certain* he'd seen something, and for Clark, that was more than enough.

Clark believed, with all his heart, that maybe something lingered out here, amidst the scent of decaying leaves and melting ice and thick loam. If he couldn't believe that...well, what even was the purpose of all of this? Belief didn't have to be *seen* to be *known*. It was a feeling, deep in your gut, an understanding that the world held some of its secrets close, and maybe, just maybe, it would share a sliver of them every now and again.

If you were in the right place at the right time, the world would give you some kind of insight into what happens after someone you loved passed.

That was what kept Clark going. He'd never seen his parents after their deaths, but he *believed* they were near. And every glimmer of ghostly light in the woods, every patch of cold air in a warm room? Those were opportunities to maybe see them one more time.

And this mad dash through the woods with Jasper at his side, their breaths heaving, their flashlights bobbing? One more chance. One more hope. One more wish for luck on his side.

"There!" Jasper whispered hoarsely, pointing west. "Did you see it?"

Clark paused to swallow hard and peer into the thick darkness. Seconds passed, and with each one, his heart beat a little faster.

There

A flicker of light, ghost-green and thin. But it was *real*.

"What should we do? It's just...hovering there," Jasper whispered in his ear.

"I'm not sure," Clark whispered back. "But maybe we should try to get closer? Whatever it is, I don't want to scare it." Jasper didn't move, though, so Clark squeezed his hand for reassurance. "It's okay. These entities? They don't hurt anyone. It's like..." He swallowed hard, trying to force his brain and heart and lungs onto the same wavelength. "They're just making their presence known. Nothing else."

"So, we should just watch?"

"I think so."

The ghostly light bobbed a little bit, as if acknowledging them. Clark heard Jasper suck in a breath. He was biting the inside of his own cheek and would gnaw it bloody if he didn't stop, so Clark let out his own shaky breath as they watched.

The light shifted again, its glow diminishing. And then like a candle being snuffed out, it was gone.

With it, Clark felt something leave him, too; as if he'd been on edge all night and that little light had taken a bit of him with it. But it wasn't a loss - Clark felt relieved, happy, even if he could already feel exhaustion nipping at his heels.

Their trip had been a *success*.

Clark knew he'd be rolling this entire night around in his head for months to come, wondering and hoping that little ghost light had been someone close to him. He'd never know for certain, but the hope was indeed a thing of feathers and lightness and it's what he would hold dear for the rest of his life.

Clark was certain they were near.

Every encounter was a bit of hope he'd sew into his heart.

"You okay?" Clark whispered. When Jasper turned toward him with an expression of pure awe on his face, Clark took that as a win. "It can be a lot, I know. Nothing really prepares you for your first sighting, or even your second –"

Jasper pulled Clark to him, a look of aching sweetness in his eyes, and swooped down to kiss him. The tension that vibrated through them both bled out into something softer now, and it made Clark shudder while Jasper gripped his shoulders. There was the taste of night air on Jasper's lips, a shiver of excitement and adrenaline down his spine, and Clark held on with everything he had. This kiss bore the hesitation of newness, but it promised something more.

"Jasper."

"Shit." Jasper pulled back, eyes wide. "I'm so sorry. I think I got caught up in the moment."

Clark yanked him back down, trying to not sound desperate. "Kiss me again. Please?"

"Well, since you asked..."

Slow and soft. Like molasses in his veins. Every touch, every slide of Jasper's lips on his made Clark grip him harder, and in return, Jasper kept him close, held him tight. Their layers made things strangely chaste but Clark didn't care. He'd wanted Jasper for some time and tonight, things felt *right*.

If he could easily believe in ghost lights and trails and the thinning of some otherworldly veil, Clark could easily believe that he and Jasper were supposed to be here, together, in this moment. Sharing kisses that were growing increasingly slick and wanton, leaving Clark to moan while Jasper held him.

And then Clark had a wild idea and he started to giggle. Maybe it was the exaltation of the moment, maybe it was the heady sensation of *knowing*, maybe it was Jasper's kisses. But it made him laugh and left Jasper staring at Clark, a smile spreading across his handsome face.

"I feel so happy," Clark said as he wound his fingers into the tassels on Jasper's scarf. "When you go on these hunts, it's always with the hope of seeing something. But I don't think anyone really believes they're going to see something even one percent of the time. It's the *hope* that keeps us coming back. And then we did see something and you looked at me like you couldn't believe what just happened..." Clark took a breath, took a moment to gaze up at Jasper. "You kissed me. I've wanted that for so long."

"You have?" Jasper slid his palms under Clark's jaw and Clark fought not to whine at the contact. "You should have said something. Or maybe I should have. I've wanted to do that for a while, too."

"Okay, good. Then we're on the same page. Let's go back to the campsite."

"And?"

Clark liked the way a wicked gleam formed in Jasper's eyes. It made him feel like he wasn't stepping out of bounds when he said, "And come to my tent. Yours is terrible, and I'm too fond of you to let you freeze."

An hour later

"I don't think some duct tape is going to fix that," Clark said when Jasper ducked into his tent to examine the tear near the roof. "Yikes."

"All the better that a very handsome and kind man is going to share his tent with me," Jasper said with a wink.

It had started to drizzle as they neared their campsite, and Clark was all the more grateful that he'd packed extra camping blankets and towels. The weather was notorious for jumping several degrees and raining at the drop of a hat. And he couldn't exactly leave Jasper to shiver, could he?

Once they got Jasper's gear moved over to his tent, Clark handed Jasper the blankets and towels and set about drying himself off, moving to the other side of the tent to give Jasper some space. No one, even someone he'd kissed minutes ago, needed another person up in their space while trying to peel off wet gear. And with sweat and rain making his entire body feel downright soggy, Clark set about getting his own kit off. The sooner he could be dry, the better. Thankfully, the tent had a nice sturdy floor and the campsite was level, so they could take their boots off. Clark moved his to a corner, far away from their bedrolls, and pulled his hat off as he turned back. Ugh, his hair was all damp and it needed a good towel dry.

"Wow."

Clark straightened, his hat dangling from one hand. "What?"

The blatant *hunger* in Jasper's eyes stopped Clark dead in his tracks. He'd taken off his hat as well, and his hair was loose, trailing over his shoulders. Jasper had managed to wriggle out of his thick sweater and was down to a black long-sleeved thermal and his hiking pants, looking all the more like the movie version of someone who had just come in from the rain. The sight of him made Clark's mouth go dry.

"Maybe I sound ridiculous but you..." Jasper came closer, his steps slow but sure. Clark couldn't move, didn't want to, not with the way Jasper was looking at him. "You look incredible."

Clark gave a weak laugh. "I look like a drowned rat."

"No, no. Not at all. You look like someone needs to care for you. Warm you up."

Part of Clark wanted to sink into the ground; just melt into a puddle and let Jasper have his way. The other part of him wanted – no, *needed* – to show his appreciation for Jasper's boldness. So, Clark chose action, tossing his hat to the side and plucking up a dry towel, holding it out in silent offering.

Jasper was a quick study.

The way he stalked toward Clark would have been enough to set Clark's blood on fire, but that fine set of lips curled up into a smile and those long-fingered musician's hands took the towel to bring it to Clark's head. And then gently place it on top. "Oh, like this then?"

Clark glared up at Jasper from under the towel, biting back a laugh. Jasper looked so serious but his lips were twitching. "I prefer a more hands-on approach -"

Jasper swooped down and kissed him while pulling Clark closer with the ends of the towel. Clark sighed into the kiss and looped his arms around Jasper's neck. Jasper's palms were sliding down Clark's back and their kiss was gentle and sweet and it all made Clark's head spin pleasantly.

And then Jasper palmed the back of Clark's head, fingers sinking into his wet curls. His other hand slid further down, pushing their hips together. "Oh, fuck," Clark whispered before Jasper claimed his mouth with a sudden urgency. He tangled his fingers in Jasper's hair and held on while Jasper tasted him. Held Clark in place so he could explore and learn, so he could map Clark's spine with his fingertips and suck on Clark's tongue and leave them both breathless. *Aching. Wanting.*

"Should we move to..." Clark pointed to their bedrolls and Jasper grinned, but didn't stop stroking Clark's back. A thumb traced around the outside of Clark's ear and he shivered. "Keep doing that and I'm going to melt," Clark warned.

"I don't see how that's a bad thing. Unless you don't want to melt," Jasper said. "Then I'd be happy to participate."

"I didn't bring any uh...supplies," Clark said, trying to not sound panicked. *Please don't let that be the thing that fucks this up.*

To Clark's massive relief, Jasper said, "It's not always about the physical act. Not for me, at least." The kiss Jasper placed at the bend of Clark's jaw made Clark suck in a breath. "I would love to keep doing this." He placed another kiss, this time just below Clark's ear. Clark tried not to whimper at the contact.

Then Jasper dropped his voice into a whisper and said, "I'm also very good with my hands, if that's of interest."

Clark let out some muttered expletive – he had no idea what he actually said, but Jasper seemed to get the hint. Grinning, Jasper pulled Clark over to their bedrolls, under which Clark had placed an air mattress. It would be a tight fit, but that didn't seem to bother Jasper. He rolled onto his side as Clark shuffled blankets and pillows around, and the moment Clark's back hit the mattress, Jasper laid a gentle hand in the middle of his chest and said, "Tell me what you want."

So many things.

My fevered dreams don't hold a candle to how you're looking at me now, all shadows and passion and damp hair, smelling like the pine needles we crushed under our boots hiking up that hill.

Clark stared up at Jasper and let his touch linger on Jasper's warm cheek. Jasper pushed into the touch, eyes fluttering shut. He looked *besotted.* "Touch me like there's no one here but us. No other hunters, no campers, no one for miles," Clark whispered. "Touch me like I matter."

Clark awoke when the first rays of morning changed the light in the tent, casting through the orange and gray nylon that had kept them dry all night. He glanced over to see Jasper curled up on his side, head pillowed on his arm, blonde hair gone frizzy from the damp.

Clark never wanted to leave. It was perfect.

Just as he considered closing his eyes once more, Jasper stirred, yawning and stretching like a cat. "Are you staring at me?" Jasper asked, cracking one eye open. "Well, I never."

Clark chuckled. "Don't look so good in the morning and I won't stare."

"I'll make a note."

Jasper extended a hand out and Clark took it, letting Jasper tug him back down, spooning him close until they were plastered together, back to chest. Clark gave a fleeting thought to how gross he must be, but it wasn't as though Jasper was in any better condition. And really, did it matter? Those weird little hang-ups didn't seem to matter one bit – not here, not now.

"I have never enjoyed myself so thoroughly as I did last night," Jasper purred in Clark's ear. "Everything was perfect."

Clark's throat went dry. "Yeah. Yeah, I thought so, too."

Jasper hummed softly, the sound resonating down Clark's spine. "I think I dreamed of that ghost light, or ghost trail."

Clark turned to face Jasper, the air mattress creaking as he shifted. "Really? Just about the light we saw?"

"That and…" Jasper's eyes were soft from sleep but he looked thoughtful, lips pursed and eyebrows drawn down. "I don't know how to describe it. It was a feeling more than anything else. Like…contentment. Like whatever, or whoever, that light had been was *happy* we'd been there to acknowledge it. Maybe I'm delusional, but it felt *real*."

Lying on an air mattress in the middle of a vast forest, after everything they'd done and said and experienced, Clark felt like he was seeing Jasper for the first time.

Belief. *Real belief.*

He'd no doubt that Jasper *wanted* to see something, to experience something in those woods, or during any of his other ghost hunting trips, but now it had the impact of an anvil through glass. Jasper bore that same look Clark had worn the first time he'd seen something after his father's death.

It was the kind of belief that could lead people into something new, something *more*. And Clark was honored he'd been with Jasper when it happened.

"You're not delusional," Clark said as he tucked a strand of hair behind Jasper's ear. "Something changed. Maybe in you, maybe in the world. Maybe both. But you'll never be the same, and we think that's such a scary thing. But it doesn't have to be that way."

"Would you…" Jasper reached over to run the backs of his fingers across Clark's cheek. "Do you think you could help me figure it out?"

Clark leaned into him, tangling their fingers together as their lips met. "I would love that."

Chapter Thirteen

Bren awoke with Elodie curled up next to her. The night rushed back in a swirl of color and sound and sensation, all tied to the woman sleeping beside her.

"I don't do sex on first dates," Elodie said, her lips curling into a grin as they broke apart from their kiss. "But I have a feeling you're cool with that."

Bren shook her head and matched Elodie's grin with one of her own. "Doesn't bother me. At all. Honestly...sex is fine. But it's not the goal. Connection is more important to me."

Elodie's gorgeous eyes flashed with understanding. "I'm so into that," she said, leaning in to brush another kiss across Bren's lips.

The knot that had formed in Bren's chest released all at once and in her relief, she kissed back hard. Elodie made a muffled sound and gripped Bren with strong fingers, but she let Bren steer their kiss, slow it down until they were pressing their foreheads together and breathing in sync. "Connection," Bren whispered.

They'd fallen asleep watching a movie in Bren's bedroom, making comments on the ridiculous plot and overacting. Bren had loved every minute of it. Elodie made her feel seen and wanted, but it was never *too much*, never forcing her into a situation where she'd have to firmly bow out.

Bren would be lying if having Elodie so close to her right now wasn't affecting her physically. She could watch the rise and fall of Elodie's chest, feel the warmth of her skin, the softness of the hand resting on her stomach, and know that if things went right, she could have all of that and more. Kissing Elodie was like candy, sweet and addictive. And Bren could imagine the two of them fumbling out of their clothes together, even if it was just to touch.

But the pull of their connection was the sexiest thing Bren could imagine right now. Elodie loved plants and nature the way she did. Loved digging her hands in the dirt and seeing tender green shoots push up to catch the sunlight and the rain. Elodie liked the rain and the cold, neither of which ever bothered Bren.

Funny, she thought as she stared at Elodie's gently fluttering eyelids and slightly parted lips, *water and plants are how we met. Those things, those everlasting, beautiful, fragile, incredible things brought us together. I wonder if we can withstand the way they do. Can any of us withstand time like they do, though?*

In times of confusion and emotion, Bren's brain liked to walkabout, as Clark called it. For all her gentle teasing on how her brother could jump from topic to topic with the passion of a true bibliophile, Bren's brain liked to find the trees, or the forest, depending on the situation.

In Elodie, Bren saw both. And it terrified her.

Bren laid her head back on the pillow, pulled Elodie closer, and let sleep carry her away once more.

#

The next day

From: Elodie That was the best date ever.

From: Bren I'm glad you enjoyed it. It wasn't...too basic?

From: Elodie BASIC??? Bren, you made me dinner. We watched a crappy movie.

From: Elodie And do I need to mention the kissing??!! It was...incredible. You've made me happier than I've been in years. *Years*, Bren.

From: Bren Okay so...when do you want to come over and reassure me?

From: Elodie I KNEW IT. I knew there was an angle! Well, far be it from me to refuse the invitation. I've got class Mon-Wed, and today's cleaning/chores/oh shit I have papers to grade. How's your Thursday looking?

From: Bren Thurs looks perfect.

The sound of tires on gravel caught Bren's ear, and she got up off the ratty sofa in the main house to go greet Clark. He'd texted her earlier in the morning to let her know he was coming home. As curious as she was to how his trip had been, Bren was far more interested in hearing how things with Jasper had gone. Because her brother had it bad for this guy, and watching Clark nurse a broken heart just couldn't be in the cards for them. It couldn't. They'd been dealt enough blows recently.

"Need help with your stuff?" Bren asked after sticking her head out the front door. Clark grinned at her, looking pale and tired except for the splash of pink across his cheeks. *Interesting.*

"You are a saint," Clark said as he waved her to him. "Thank you."

"Like I'm going to let you struggle."

Clark narrowed his eyes at her, paused, then laughed. "You just want dirt."

Bren chose to ignore that, reaching out to brush a bit of dried mud off his jacket. "Speaking of dirt…"

"I know, I'm gross. Give me twenty, and I'll tell you everything."

Bren could count on one hand the number of times Clark had "witnessed" something supposedly supernatural. At first, she had thought his obsession would fade out with the whimsy of childhood; she'd always been stoic, even when she was young, but Clark jumped in puddles and called them oceans, preferring imaginary friends and the company of books over kids their age. Not that she had fared any better, being tall and good at sports and math. Neither of them had really matched with any gender ideals.

But when Clark claimed to have seen a ghost right after their father passed away when they were ten, and then again at fifteen? Again around his twenty-seventh birthday? After Mom died? And then now? Maybe it wasn't whimsy.

Clark's gaze on her, steady and even, seemed to ask: *I believe, why don't you?*

And for once, Bren didn't have a good answer.

"It was a ghost trail, Bren," Clark finally said as he gripped the pillow he held tightly to his chest. The sight of him curled up like that made him look a decade younger, and it forced Bren's already aching heart to hurt a little more. "Jasper's researched the shit out of them, and *we saw one*. It didn't really lead anywhere, but all we know, maybe it did. Maybe where it stopped had been a house at one point, or a farm. Maybe someone was buried right under our feet, so far down that they'd been reclaimed by the woods. But we saw it."

Bren stared at her brother, her twin, her closest friend and only family left, and asked a very simple question. "Do you think it was one of them? Or both?"

That question seemed to throw Clark for a loop. It wasn't completely surprising, given Bren had never been so direct about the possibility before. Most of the time if Clark approached it, she'd deflect and move on. In her worst moments, Bren let her anger and impatience get in the way, using Clark's belief to call him into question.

How can you believe that when your whole career is around facts and research?

It makes no sense, Clark. They're gone and that's it.

Why would they come back? To watch us suffer? To watch us mourn? That doesn't sound like Mom and Dad at all. They weren't cruel. You're just grieving.

After time dripped in the silence between them, Clark finally replied. "No. I don't think it was them. But I think it was something, maybe someone. Just a tiny piece of something asking for attention."

"Then it found it. Because it found you." Bren put her hand over his and squeezed hard. "And you have way too big of a heart to be ignored."

Clark snorted but the sound was weak. "I just got home. Don't make me cry."

"Okay then..." She shifted closer and leaned into the back of the couch, her left arm up on the scrollwork wood running along the top. "Tell me about Jasper."

That got Bren a grin. "If you tell me about Elodie."

Chapter Fourteen

Two months later

"No one told me the room came with such...gorgeous company."

Clark leaned against the door frame and shot Jasper a smile. He hoped it was a little sultry, especially given the way Jasper was staring at him.

Or maybe it was the long emerald green dressing gown Clark had wrapped himself in, only a hint of shoulder peeking out as the fabric slipped down. He'd taken to wearing his father's wedding ring on a short silver chain, and Clark wasn't unaware of how he must look in green and silver, the colors bringing out the pale flush to his skin and the tiny bit of gray starting at his temples.

There was hunger in Jasper's gaze. Hunger in the twitch of his fingers on his thigh. Clark knew the loose black pants Jasper wore were incredibly soft. The man had an appreciation for soft fabrics, like Clark did, and seeing those pants on his lean frame did something to Clark's insides. Hopefully it was the same sensual twist Jasper was feeling at the moment.

"Come here," Jasper growled, beckoning with the crook of a single finger. Clark walked over to him, feeling as though he were floating, and let Jasper pull him down to the bed. The dressing gown slipped a little more and Jasper kissed what was revealed.

"You shiver so beautifully when I do that," Jasper whispered into Clark's ear. "So sensitive here. But so cunning, teasing me like that."

"As if I'm...*ah, Jasper*...not going to wear your incredibly thoughtful gift." Clark managed the words between gasping pants as Jasper continued to kiss and lick along the top of his shoulder. Jasper was *incredibly* tactile, and Clark had no problem reaping the reward of it.

Jasper drew his face up with a hand under his chin, thumb on Clark's lip indenting so gently. It made Clark want to suck it into his mouth. "Happy birthday," Jasper whispered before claiming Clark's mouth in a kiss.

They stayed in the room on the first night, preferring to keep out of the spring rain and hope for sunshine the following morning. Jasper had rented them a room at a small bed and breakfast in the Upper Peninsula. Four days, a long weekend of relaxation and tangling their legs between the sheets and then, on the third day, visiting the ghost towns of the area. There were quite a few, given how the area had been built up and then fallen into disrepair and eventual abandonment rather quickly. All due to the copper trade in the mid and late 19th century. Clark had visited a few of the towns before, but he'd never really stopped to consider all their history.

And getting out of town, even for a few days, was a very good excuse to spend as much time between historical hikes in bed with his boyfriend. The trip had been his idea, but the dressing gown had been Jasper's surprise.

The gown got trapped under them as Jasper rolled Clark onto his back. "No, wait, the gown," Clark moaned into Jasper's mouth. His body craved this man, but Clark didn't want the delicate fabric to wrinkle.

"Here," Jasper said while helping Clark take it off. "You're beautiful in everything but that green makes you look..." Jasper paused to run his palms down Clark's shoulders, over his chest, all while Clark sank into those touches. "Ethereal. Timeless."

The compliment, and the way Jasper looked when he said it, hit Clark square in the chest. He was splayed out under Jasper, naked and writhing in the sheets, with the sudden realization that he had Jasper's undivided attention. It felt *so good* to be wanted like this, to be seen and touched and loved unconditionally.

"Touch me," Clark said in a hoarse whisper. "Please."

"Anything," Jasper replied before he swept Clark into a searing kiss.

The next day, Clark and Jasper stood on the grounds of what once was a thriving copper mining village and soaked in the morning sun. "My god, it's so quiet out here," Jasper said as they stared out over the empty spot where the village had been. "Did we pass any cars on the way up here?"

Clark shook his head. "Not a single one." Overhead, a crow cawed loudly, the sound reverberating through the empty space and off the trees in the distance. It sounded like it carried for miles. "Should we walk around a little?"

"Yes. It's too beautiful to not explore some."

Clark's research before the trip had let him plot out a dozen sites to visit. Some still had what could be called an active town, rambling brick and wood buildings standing where clapboard houses had once been built. A few towns even had small historical centers for tourists.

But where they drove to this morning was completely void of evidence of the past, save a few stone remnants of buildings and one lonely, dilapidated well.

In the daylight, this abandoned town felt like hollow memories just waiting to be discovered. It was hard to imagine an entire village standing there, the houses built close to each other and a smelter installed right near the center of town. There were a few artistic illustrations of the town in a library database, and a few journal entries from town residents. Those voices didn't reach here, though, in the lukewarm spring sun as they gazed out over grass and trees and mud.

As Clark and Jasper explored, they talked. About everything. They'd done this so often of late, Clark had quickly lost track of trying to catalog their interests and dislikes, instead learning to trust the ebb and flow of it all. Jasper, as it turned out, was a giant gaming nerd and could completely wreck Clark in PvP matches on his game console. Clark thought it incredibly endearing that this tall, handsome, talented man sometimes wanted to wind down the day by obliterating his teams with the most graceful button-mashing he'd ever seen.

Jasper was rambling on about the new battle strategy game he'd seen when Clark tripped over it. "What the..."

Jasper had caught him by the arm, a worried look on his face, before saying, "Was it a root?"

"No, it didn't give at all." Clark knelt to brush aside forest detritus. "Oh, it was a rock. But it looks weird."

"That's not a rock, Clark." Jasper knelt beside him and together they removed the rest of the dirt and old leaves and pine needles. "My god. It's a gravestone."

"No way." Clark could barely breathe.

Jasper looked around, peering into the dense forest that was coming to life with the warmer temperatures of spring. Assessing. "I wonder if there'd been a graveyard here or nearby at some point. Maybe all the rain and snow moved this one."

"Maybe. Here, help me stand it up."

Together they lifted the thick slab of unpolished stone. It had been white or near it at some point, but time had eroded the stone's color into a milky gray. Part of the rounded top had broken off, leaving a jagged edge on the right side. After a few minutes of wiping off the dirt, Clark could finally read the inscription:

Louisa Anna Michaels
Beloved sister and daughter
1832-1842

"A child," Jasper said, his voice thick with emotion.

Carefully, Jasper pulled more mud and pine needles from the worn inscription. "I wonder who she was."

"Maybe we can find records of her once we're back home."

Clark smiled at him. "I'd like that. We should take some pictures, maybe prop this up against a tree?"

"Agreed. There's no telling where her grave is now but we can at least leave the stone somewhere someone else might see it." Jasper helped Clark to his feet and they both stared down at the old gravestone. "Poor thing," Jasper said while lacing his fingers through Clark's. It felt good to have Jasper anchor him down, give him the strength and time to think.

"I bet I can reach someone at the state library, see if they have any records," Clark said. "It's the least I can do."

They propped the stone up against a thick oak tree, out of the wind as much as possible. Jasper took several pictures of the stone and Clark made notes in his field notebook. He didn't want to forget any of this, didn't want to forget little Louisa's name.

Eventually, the day wore on and Jasper pulled Clark back to their car for a break and lunch. "Do you want to go back to our room and rest for a bit?" Jasper asked as they bit into sandwiches and fruit the bed and breakfast had graciously prepared for them. "Dig into who Louisa was?"

Clark shook his head. "No, let's keep going. I don't want to end the day with a question. We're on a mini break. No work allowed." He snatched an apple slice from Jasper's fingers and popped it into his mouth. "Not even work for the ghostly realms."

"Apple thief."

"That's an awfully strong accusation, dear."

Laughing, Jasper leaned into Clark, bumping their noses together. "I've been upgraded to *dear*, have I? I like it."

"I'm glad." When Jasper hummed into the kiss Clark stole, Clark felt it vibrate through his entire body. "You're the best, you know that?"

"I do now." Jasper kissed him again, his hands gripping Clark's waist tightly. "I love you. Two months in, and you've completely smitten me."

The shock of those words made Clark want to weep. It felt *so good*. "I love you," he whispered back, knowing that love and those passions and the things that made him and Jasper click were shared and appreciated in equal measure.

Chapter Fifteen

Two months later

"Wait, hold on, Iris. I don't think your mic's plugged in."

"I can hear her, Bren."

"Ah, shit."

Elodie laughed while Iris snickered behind her hand and said, "Language, Bren! We're live!"

Iris continued to crack up while Elodie took the reins of the show for a moment while Bren found the problem with the sound. "Hi, everyone! It's not a live show, especially not a first live show, without a few tech issues, right? So, you've all heard our voices before but you've not seen us while we record. And we're really glad you're here...wow, okay, all thousand of you."

Bren snapped her head up so fast she smacked it on the bottom of the table. The cable that had come unplugged was just within reach if she stretched a little more. "A thousand?" she croaked, disbelieving. That was an awful lot of people tuning into Pennyroyal & Mugwort's first live podcast. They'd all hoped for an audience, particularly because they were doing a live show for charity, but a thousand people was...a lot.

Bren dove forward, snatched up the cable between her thumb and index finger, and quickly plugged it in. Immediately, both sides of her headphones picked up the mics, so Bren got back in her seat and set the headphones aside. She'd only needed them for sound check and with chat confirming everyone could be heard, Bren settled in for the next two hours.

"Whew okay, I think we're good," Elodie said as Iris grinned at Bren's thumbs-up. "So again, hi everyone. We're really excited you're here, and hopefully in the name of supporting the Young Gardeners Association."

This had been part of their rehearsal the previous day, so Bren picked up where Elodie left off. The nerves that had twisted her stomach into knots hours before now slowly unraveled as she launched into the info she knew by heart. "Our goal is five thousand dollars so we can help the association send gardening boxes to schools and libraries to start their own community gardens. My brother, Clark, who works at our local library, is helping to coordinate efforts with other public libraries. And we here at Pennyroyal & Mugwort are going to work with the schools and other gardening centers. Five thousand will let us send one hundred boxes out -"

"Uh, Bren?" Iris pointed toward their donation ticker on a screen near her right elbow. "Goal met."

The chat erupted as Bren and Elodie leaned in to look. "What the hell?" Bren muttered, only catching herself after the words had slipped out. Elodie and Iris didn't even tease her about it. But there it was on the screen: over five thousand dollars raised in a matter of minutes. Most of the donations were small amounts, but the last few had been for several hundred dollars.

And the one at the top of the list was for one thousand dollars even.

"Who donated a thousand dollars?" Iris whirled around, as if she could see the person. "Anonymous donor! Dang. Well, whoever you are, you just made a lot of kids really happy."

Iris kept talking, letting the chat know about the stretch goals (the ones they hadn't advertised and never thought they'd get to use), but Bren was looking at Elodie. There were tears in her eyes and she was subtly wiping them away. Bren caught her hand and gave it a squeeze. "You okay?"

Elodie gave a watery laugh. "You know they can hear us, right?"

Bren shrugged and gestured at the screens around them. "*They* just helped us raise a bunch of money for a really good cause. I think a few tears are more than in order."

The small gaggle of her friends and family in the dining room was a sight Bren wanted to savor, so she stood in the doorway between that room and the kitchen and watched. She watched Clark smile at Jasper before he handed Havaa a glass of wine. She saw Elodie and Pierre laugh at something the new house cat, Cheese, did with a small mouse toy. None of them noticed her for several long seconds, but eventually Elodie looked her way.

Elodie, in her typical fashion, didn't just lock gazes with Bren. She *beamed*, all sunshine and newly dyed purple hair and wearing the shiny silver hoops Bren had bought her after their charity drive's success. It had been a symbol of Bren's thanks and adoration, and Elodie had understood that immediately. She wore the hoops often and Bren never had to ask if it was because Elodie felt beholden. Elodie wore them because she liked them, and Bren. Simple as that.

And while Bren hadn't ever said it out loud, she liked seeing Elodie in silver. It glittered and sparkled whenever she moved; a perfect match for Elodie's bright personality. Maybe one day Bren would be brave enough to say such things out loud.

"Get in here," Elodie said and immediately the chatter and warmth of those she loved curled up around Bren. A blanket of safety and surety, but also of togetherness. Cheese meowed at Bren as she passed and she scratched the cat between her ears, laughing as Cheese affectionately nosed at her fingers.

"I hope for your sake you don't smell like food," Clark said. "The little weirdo was licking my fingers after I ate an orange last night."

"Ew, Cheese, no," Havaa laughed. "Oranges aren't for kitties."

"I don't think she cares," Jasper said as he reached for the cat. Cheese butted up into his hand, purring loudly. "She's a bit of an equal opportunity affection and food chaser."

"Says the one who feeds her table scraps, which is not good for her!" Clark tried to sound like he was reprimanding Jasper, but it came out as more affectionately exasperated than anything else.

Pierre motioned them all over to the table, where he'd set up a massive board game, one he promised would be easy to learn. "This looks a little complicated," Bren said as she surveyed the brightly colored pieces and at least two dozen game tiles laid out in a T-grid. "Pierre, I swear —"

"It *is* easy!" Pierre protested, laughing. "I wouldn't lie about that."

As they all sat and passed around bowls of snacks and a basket of pens, Elodie nudged Bren's shoulder with hers. "This is really fun. Thank you for inviting me."

"Yeah, of course." Under the table, Bren put her hand on Elodie's knee. A gentle, reassuring touch, one she hoped said *thank you* in a way her words couldn't convey properly. "I'm just really glad you're here."

"I wouldn't miss it."

Also By Halli Starling

About The Author

Halli Starling (she/they) is a queer author, librarian, gamer, editor, and nerd. *The Way We Wind* is her sixth book. Her work can be found on hallistarlingbooks.com and she's on Twitter and Instagram @hallistarling.

Printed in Great Britain
by Amazon

23411276R00089